Chrysanthemum Palace

The Princess Chronicles

This book is a work of fiction. Any reference to real events, people, or places are used fictitiously. Other names, characters, places and incidents are the products of the author's imagination. Any resemblance to actual events, locales, or persons; living or dead, is entirely coincidental.

CHRYSANTHEMUM PALACE

THE PRINCESS CHRONICLES

MORGANA SINCLAYR

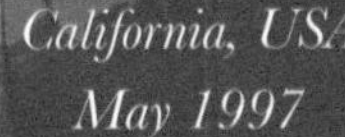

California, USA
May 1997

Just like any other Saturday afternoon, the sun blazed high in the skies of California, but May 31, 1997, was a day that would never be forgotten.

"This is only temporary. Until the day she turns eighteen, Eleanor Aurora will live a normal life. Then she'll be allowed to make her own decision." Hironori Yamamoto was not a typical college graduate. Instead of a fresh-faced graduate excited at the possibilities for the future, Hironori shouldered a large responsibility in his home country. On this day, he was tasked with making preparations for illegitimate child Eleanor Aurora Yamamoto to be raised by his ex-girlfriend's family, who, unfortunately, was suffering from the loss of their daughter to a traumatic childbirth.

With the harsh condition of no one around the girl ever mentioning anything about her father, young Eleanor will grow up with no knowledge of her true heritage, culture, or family—and, most importantly, the prestigious title she holds in a country far east.

CHAPTER ONE

IKAN

May 18, 2015

"Kids grow up so fast," most adults say. When I was younger, I thought this statement was the furthest from the truth. Time seems to pass by slowly, inching forward day by day during one's childhood. It's when one begins middle school that life seems to go by in a whirlwind. Before you know it, you'll be standing in front of the high school you used to pass by on your way to kindergarten as an eighteen-year-old senior who has no idea what she wants to do with the rest of her life.

This is the best way to describe my current situation. With my pink kitten ear headphones blasting a catchy K-pop tune into my ears, there I stood in front of Valley High amongst the other offenders who had dared to come to class late. Disrupting my deep thoughts, the school bell rang loudly, signaling that class had begun. Realizing that I was late for the fifth time this month, I sighed loudly as I raced up the steps. My feet picked up speed down the main corridor, my curly dark brown lavender-dipped locks secured in ponytails trailing behind me. What's my excuse this time for my tardiness? My phone alarm—set to "Lovely Day"—not going off like it was supposed to. Luckily, I made it to class just in time for attendance.

Mrs. Williams paid no attention to me while I took a seat at the desk farthest from the front of the room. Some of my fellow classmates softly snickered as they looked back at me, knowing very well I was toast. Mrs. Williams was known to be a stickler—nothing got past her. Taking out a yellow number two pencil, I looked straight ahead as my teacher recited the directions, ignoring my nosey classmates. Today was May 18, 2015, the day of my calculus test in first period—and the anniversary of my birth.

While papers and bubble sheets were passed down to each student from row to row, I couldn't help but think about the many questions I had that had long been left unanswered by my grandmother and other relatives.

"Ms. Yamamoto?" Ms. Williams bellowed from the front of the room, snapping me out of my daydream. Some of my peers' heads turned away from their tests, glancing back in curiosity as I quickly straightened myself at my desk.

"Yes?"

I knew I wouldn't be let off the hook this time. Waiting for the hard lashing to come from my teacher's tongue, Ms. Williams released an inaudible sigh, as if attempting to suppress her irritability. "See me after class."

I guess today won't be so lovely after all.

"So Williams finally gave you detention, huh, Eleanor?" my friend Anna asked. "You finally got a rebel streak in ya!" Anna Russo and I had been friends since the first grade; we were inseparable! According to her, we were Valley High's most fashionable duo. A second-generation Italian American, she's always had an amazing sense of style. With her natural knack for illustration and design, two of Anna's pieces were featured in our school's fashion showcase last semester.

As usual, she was dressed to the nines, wearing a thrifted pink-and-blue vintage letterman jacket, a matching pleated skirt that she probably rolled up to make shorter, loose knee-high socks, and white sneakers. She wore her bottle-blonde locks in loose curls that hung to her shoulders. Anna stood at the petite stature of five feet three, proudly sporting a mild Valley Girl tan, and had brown almond-shaped eyes.

We were headed to the courtyard to meet with the Bianchi brothers, who were supposed to bring us burgers, fries, and a drink from Roscoe's Burger across the street. However, on our way to our daily meetup spot, we found many people congregating around the fence, observing a skirmish between the Costello twins . . . and the Bianchi brothers.

The Costello twins were seniors from the west side, the upper-middle-class part of town, while the Bianchis resided in the newly established projects Anna and I lived down the road from. The Bianchi's and Costello's feud was kind of like that of the Montagues and Capulets, but not *quite* that tragic. They fought often due to their younger siblings in middle school, who were currently dating. Since the Bianchi family business competed with the Costellos' grocery chain, the two had always butted heads.

"That small stunt you and your brother pulled the other day was out of line!" Robbin Costello spat while unbuttoning his navy blue blazer and throwing it to the ground without a care. His hazel eyes burned straight into the eldest Bianchi's, Rodney.

Rodney Bianchi was a senior and, unfortunately for Anna, he was also her boyfriend. Rodney's gray eyes darkened as he gazed back at Robbin, showing no sign of intimidation. As usual, he had to make a smart remark. "And what are you going to do about it?"

At that moment, Rodney shoved Robbin onto the cold hard concrete pavement, officially starting the fight. The crowd watched with enthusiasm, cheering while taking one or the other's side. Anna, sick of seeing her boyfriend get into trouble, started pushing through the crowd, attempting to break up the skirmish.

"Cut it out, Rodney!" she exclaimed with her Italian accent becoming stronger while jumping in front of him before Robbin, who was a heavyweight boxer, could knock him out—something that had happened just yesterday, to Anna's dismay.

Rodney, who never thought about the consequences before he started swinging, lightly pushed his girlfriend out of the way. "Anna, stay out of this! Take Elle and wait at our meeting spot."

"No!" Anna protested while placing herself between the two again. "I'm not allowing you to get hurt again."

Robbin's younger brother, who was standing near his older sib, decided to intervene too. "Just this once, I think you should listen to your girl, Bianchi. She seems to have a pretty good head on her shoulders, unlike yourself."

Rodney's eyes shifted over to his younger bro, Ricky, then back to his girlfriend, who had a determined look on her face. "Bro, sit this one out and give the girls their food! I'll meet you guys when I finish up over here."

Ricky looked over at Anna, who still wasn't budging, and grabbed her clenched hand. "Let's go!"

Anna snatched her hand away from Ricky, muttering something that I didn't understand in Italian. By the look on Ricky's face, whatever she said wasn't pleasant. "Come on, girl, these two *idiotas* are making me hungry," she grumbled to me. Anna and I followed Ricky to our nearby table, leaving Rodney to fight solo as he had requested.

"UGH! I CAN'T BELIEVE THEY'RE DOING IT AGAIN," ANNA SAID, SOUNDing über pissed.

"Boys will be boys." I shrugged while taking a sip of my soda.

"Well, Elle, I guess you'll be in good company during detention today," commented Ricky as we watched the principal break up the two boys. *Again.* Rodney was in bad shape, but at least this time he had done a little damage to Robin.

"So, got any plans after detention?" asked Anna. "If you're not busy, the guys and I were going to drop by Mixter's. SHINee just released their new album today!"

I put down my messenger bag to open up my rusty old locker, taking out my binder plastered with stickers of my favorite member, Onew. "Oh, yeah, I totally forgot! Hopefully, we can snag one before everything sells out. Mixter's is the only place in this small town that carries K-Pop merch."

"I know, right?" Anna replied. "I miss when the music we liked was considered niche and geeky. Back then, it was SO much easier shopping for merch!"

"Same, but then again, if K-Pop was still considered niche, our options for getting SHINee's new album would be one, ordering from South Korea and paying the expensive shipping fees, or two, traveling all the way to Korea Town to get a copy."

"Speaking of Korea Town, it's been a while since we visited. We should take a trip this weekend! What do ya' say Elle?" The girl proposed. "Yeah, we can all go. I'll ask Rodney if he can take us," Ricky offered.

"Sounds fun! I just have to check in with Auntie first. Y'all know how she is. " I replied. "We know," both said in unison.

IT TOOK MULTIPLE OFFENSES, BUT I HAD FINALLY LANDED MY SPOT IN the school library for detention. Having a strict disciplinarian as my aunt and legal guardian, for the first time in my life I wasn't looking forward to going home, knowing a tongue-lashing awaited upon my arrival. With my phone in the librarian's desk like all the other teenage "convicts," I passed the time with my head on the table before me, allowing my mind to roam freely, daydreaming, wandering.

Ever since I could remember, my Aunt Carol and the rest of my relatives had always been very vague whenever I inquired about my mother, the relationship between my parents, or what my father was like. Last night, Aunt Carol had done the same thing over dinner when I tried asking again. According to my family, when my parents were driving home from the hospital after my birth, they were killed on impact in a fatal accident, leaving me as the sole survivor of the crash and leaving my aunt with the responsibility of raising me.

Despite not knowing much about my parents, Aunt Carol was still a great mother to me. She took me on vacations every spring break while in primary school, enrolled me in the best finishing schools for proper grooming, and, during the summer months, signed me up for traditional dance lessons. She truly tried her best to raise an intelligent, well-rounded child. Despite our modest middle-class lifestyle, she provided for us by working as a journalist for our local newspaper. The majority of my extracurricular activities were quite costly, and I was incredibly grateful for my experiences, as they had given me many fond memories.

As I was reminiscing about the years past, the bell finally rang, bringing me back to reality as we were released from detention. Besides the librarian, it was only Rodney and I left.

"Hey, Elle, are you coming with us to Mixter's? Since I got my license now, Dad's finally letting me borrow his Civic."

"Ohh, sounds tempting! Unfortunately, I gotta get back. You know, to delete the voicemail the school left regarding me being sent to detention before my aunt gets home."

"Ahh, right, I forgot your Aunt Carol still uses that old landline. She's so old-fashioned," he said, bursting into laughter. "My parents never bat an eye anymore. Pretty much a regular here at this point."

I shook my head in disbelief at the boy sporting the black eye he'd earned earlier. "I can imagine. Tell Anna to pick up a copy of *Odd* for me pretty please? I'll definitely pay her back!"

He raked fingers through his silky wavy raven locks. "I'll let her know!"

"Thanks, bruh!"

Taking his leave, we parted ways for the day.

"You know, Yamamoto, I was quite surprised seeing your name on the roster today," said Ms. White, the librarian, in her proper English accent while handing me back my mobile phone.

"Yeah . . ." I said, not wanting to think much of the matter. Before meeting my tribe, I used to spend most of my lunch hours in the school library, surrounded by books of both fictional and real-life stories. That had been a daily ritual of mine since I started at Valley High from day one, so naturally Ms. White and I were pretty close. Knowing me as well as she did, the petite woman looked at me now with her piercing blue eyes like she wanted a better explanation.

I released a huge sigh. "It won't happen again. I've just been in deep thought lately—"

"About your past?" My reply was a silent nod. Ms. White briefly stepped away to grab a book tucked away under her desk in a drawer. "Have you ever heard of the phrase 'Ignorance is bliss,' Elle?"

"Of course." As one of the younger teachers, Ms. White was someone I'd always felt comfortable talking with—I figured she was about thirty-four—but I wondered what she was getting at.

"There are times that I don't wish to remember my past, but just this once, I'll share my story with you." Lifting the cover of the black book, Ms. White flipped through many pages as her sleek blonde hair fell in front of her face, finally pulling out a small photo of a man and woman who shared a resemblance with her. "Meet my mum and dad, a domestic and factory worker. My father was a good husband to my mother, and a loving father to myself and my two younger brothers."

"Well, what's wrong with that?"

"There's a turning point. One year, my father's workplace was laying off many of its employees; it was only a matter of time until it was my father's turn. That was a very dark time. In order to keep his sanity, my father turned to alcohol and his cigarettes. It wasn't long until he began to take out his anger on my mother and me, and within weeks, the father I once knew became a complete stranger.

"One day, it went too far . . . my mother could no longer take the beatings from my father. She tried defending herself, but he was just too strong. My mother was strangled to death." Ms. White's usual cheerful smile was replaced with a cold, eerie expression. Just from seeing her face, one could tell she was stricken with grief from reliving her past.

"I had no idea . . . what happened to your dad?" I was still shocked by her mother's fate.

"He's still alive, but after that incident, I ran away from home and took my brothers with me. It's because of him I had to grow up way too fast before my time—to become a mother to two younger children on top of my educational responsibilities."

"I'm so sorry to hear that, Ms. White . . ."

"It's okay—the past is the past. Nothing can be changed, but your future is always in your hands. I remember my mum and dad and know almost everything about them, but it's the emotional scars and trauma that make me wish that I'd never know them." There was a brief pause as a heavy silence stretched over both of us for what seemed like forever. "That's why, in some ways, ignorance is bliss—because the truth sometimes only leaves pain and misery."

Ms. White's story remained heavy on my mind while walking back home from school. While I often felt unhappy knowing so little about my birth parents, maybe there was a specific reason why it was so, I reasoned. *Were my parents horrible individuals? Are they really dead like Aunt Carol and everyone else has been telling me all my life?* Some details just didn't add up, though, and after hearing Ms. White's story, I became even more suspicious about my past.

While turning onto my street, I spotted two black cars parked on the curb in front of my row home with my aunt's red car in the driveway. At this hour, she was usually still working downtown at the office. Each step I took closer to my home, situated on a hill along with two other three-story row houses, I could only guess exactly whom the two expensive-looking black cars belonged to. My heart pounded hard in my chest, and my hands started to clam up as my feet climbed the concrete stairs. *I have to think fast! Why is Auntie home so early? I just hope and pray that she didn't check the voicemail. Besides, now I have bigger fish to fry.*

Stepping up onto my front porch, I quickly reached into my bag to grab the house keys, only to have a stranger answer the door before I could put the key in the lock. The tall figure towered over me in height and had the appearance of a Secret Service agent. With a cold, stern voice, he said, "Ms. Eleanor. We've been expecting you."

If anyone else was in my current situation, I'm sure they would have yelled, screamed, or at least questioned why this peculiar balding middle-aged man looking like a secret agent was standing at their door. While there were many questions I wished to vocalize, something told me it was best to comply—to not ruffle any feathers until I could better read the situation at hand. *Hopefully, I'll return to school in one piece tomorrow morning.*

Once I entered my family's row house, my aunt was sitting in the front room surrounded by what appeared to be four other agents with the same decorum as the man who had answered the door. Still dressed properly in her work attire, my aunt appeared to be at ease, having a delightful conversation with the petite Asian woman sitting beside her as if she were speaking to an old friend.

"Auntie Carol, you're home quite early! Who are all these people?" I asked, utterly confused.

The gleeful conversation between the two women ceased as all the attention in the room was shifted to me. Both of them stood up from their seats on the couch and approached me.

"Welcome back, Elle. I know you probably have many questions, so I suggest you go on and take a seat. There's much to be explained." My aunt put her arm around me as I walked back with her to the couch, a whirlwind of questions circling in my mind.

Once I took a seat beside my aunt, the woman who had been sitting in my place cleared her throat and took her place in the center of the room, facing me.

"Hello, Ms. Eleanor. I'm Soo-Young Kim, ambassador of the country of Narea and one of the many assistants to the Imperial Family of the Chrysanthemum Throne."

"Nice to meet you . . ." I added almost inaudibly, "You're far away from home."

"Likewise," said Soo-Young, smiling warmly, lightening up the serious atmosphere. "You're quite correct, Young Miss!"

For a while, we spoke casually about a variety of subjects, so much so that I slowly became more comfortable around these individuals whom I'd just viewed as strangers in our home. "So, Ms. Kim, being an ambassador to such a large prominent country, how did you meet my aunt? You guys seem to go way back!"

Before responding to my question, the woman hesitated. She slightly glanced over to my aunt beside me for a few seconds. "Soo-Young and I had been close friends for eighteen years," answered Aunt Carol, more uneasy than usual.

Eighteen years? I was puzzled. *How come we've never met until today?*

Kim put her hand over mine which was folded neatly in my lap. "Miss Eleanor, I came here today with a message for you . . . there have been many things that your Aunt Carol has been keeping from you over the years."

"Before leaving, your father made me promise to never tell you about your past until you turned eighteen." Aunt Carol sighed deeply.

"And today's the day the truth comes out?" I asked.

Both Ms. Kim and my aunt nodded in unison. "This is going to take quite a bit of explaining. Elle, remember all of those extracurricular activities I enrolled you in when you were younger? The traditional dance classes, equestrian club, finishing school, and language camps?" Those were all precious memories of my youth. I simply nodded my head in response.

"Your aunt enrolled you in those courses to help prepare you for your life ahead. You see, Miss Eleanor, when your father met your mother, he was next in line for Narea's Chrysanthemum Throne. Since your parents were not married, they agreed that once you were born, they would give you a regular childhood outside of royal affairs until you came of age. Even after your mother died, your father still wanted to keep that promise." Kim paused, allowing my mind a moment to soak up all the information.

While I was not the best when it came to the politics of the world, from my world history courses, I believed Narea was one of the only countries left with a working hierarchy. With the Royal Family on the top of the social pyramid, Narea was run by His Supreme Royal Highness Emperor Yamamoto. Economically, the country was well-known for its tourism, pop culture, education, and technological advancements.

After the War of the East in 1985, the three prime ministers of three previously warring civilizations met at the Chrysanthemum Palace to settle their differences and promote peace. On May 3, 1985, the three countries that were once enemies merged into what the world knows today as one of the wealthiest lands in the world.

Just the idea of being part of one of the most elite families in the world sent me reeling—my mind was already flooding with questions yearning to be answered. One concern in particular jumped to the forefront. "Ms. Kim . . . may I ask who sent you to deliver me this message?"

A wide grin spread across Ms. Kim's face as well as my auntie's. After allowing my mind to connect the dots, the next words that left the ambassador's mouth confirmed everything. "Your father sent me here."

CHAPTER TWO

MEJI

May 19, 2015

R*INGGG!* My alarm blasted into the quiet, slowly getting louder and louder like every other school morning. With the darkness still blanketing my town, I slowly reached for the snooze button. After the lengthy and completely unexpected discussion last night, I found it difficult to sleep.

There was so much to think about, and after reading over the letter the ambassador had given me from my father, there was more anticipation built up inside me than ever before. While the semester was far from over, I was informed I was to collect my school records from the district and withdraw from Valley High. Within the next few months, I would be visiting my father's country for the first time and finishing up the remainder of my compulsory education at Narea's most prestigious academy for the elite.

I stretched my arms high above me, releasing an enormous yawn as I headed toward my wardrobe to retrieve my suitcase. Despite my aunt and I having taken many family trips to Utica, New York, to visit my grandparents, cousins, and close circle of friends, this would be my first time traveling abroad. I was both excited and nervous at the same time. *Just think . . . within nine hours, my life will change completely—for better or worse.*

As I packed my bags, there was a faint knock on my bedroom door. "Come in, it's open," I called.

Adorned in a Tiffany Blue satin robe and with her coiling dark-brown 'fro secured with a matching satin sash, there entered my auntie holding her daily cup of tea. Taking a seat on my silver and white vanity ottoman, she took a sip of her barley tea, watching me pack.

"Ẹ *káàrọ̀ o*, Auntie," I greeted in Yoruba.

"*Káàrọ̀ o*, my dear."

There was a heavy silence within the room. After several minutes of awkwardness, my mother's younger sister finally spoke. "Despite me knowing this day would come eventually, it's still hard to see the child that I raised as my own leave the nest."

"The sands of time drained to the bottom of the hourglass too fast," I mumbled softly. Zipping up my final bag, I put all five suitcases by the door, then took a seat on my gold metal daybed across from my aunt.

"Eleanor, remember 'All About Me Day' at your kindergarten?"

Recalling the funny, yet precious childhood memory, I released a whole-hearted giggle. "Like it was yesterday!"

In kindergarten, my teacher had assigned all thirty of her students a special day once a week. All About Me Day was every Friday morning before snack time, where one student was assigned to create a presentation to share with the class and then be interviewed by our teacher, Ms. Paisley. When the week of my presentation finally arrived, my aunt dressed me to the nines, with my waist-length dark-brown hair flat-ironed and decorated with a yellow satin ribbon that matched the yellow-and-white Sanokian dress my grandmother had sewn for my special day. That day, I proudly represented my grandparents' West African homeland.

When it was time for the interview portion, Ms. Paisley asked me, "What do you want to be when you grow up?" I looked at my auntie, who was taking photos like a proud mum, then down at my classmates sitting around my teacher and I crisscross applesauce on the carpet in our classroom. *"When I grow up, I'm going to be a princess!"*

After recalling my response, both Auntie and I burst out laughing. My five-year-old self would have been ecstatic right now.

"I wanted to tell you to come to the front yard once you're done. Everyone wants to see you off," Auntie beamed.

"Who's 'everyone'?" I asked curiously. All of our family and friends mostly live in Upstate New York.

"That's for me to know, and for you to find out!"

Both of us stood up. "Okay, after I'm finished getting dressed, I'll be right out." With a gentle nod and a brief bear hug, my aunt took her leave, shutting the door quietly behind her.

I went to my dresser and pulled out my white short-sleeved sailor blouse and an ivory-and-pink jumper skirt and quickly threw them on. Before leaving my room, I took one last look. The small twin-sized silver daybed that I'd slept in since the age of ten, the posters plastered on the walls of all my favorite singers and pop idols, and my butterfly corkboard filled to the brim with memorable photographs from my childhood . . . my room represented so much of *me.* I was somewhat happy that I'd gotten this incredible opportunity to broaden my horizons, but the other part of me felt sad about leaving everyone I knew here in Cali and Upstate.

Unpinning a photograph of me and my friends at our first concert, smiling widely in the midst of the mosh pit, I placed the Polaroid in my bag and left my old room, closing the door softly behind me.

As I opened the front door to the house, there stood my aunt, Ms. Kim, Anna and Rodney, Ms. Oshigi, and my two friends from New York, Athena and Miakoda. Ms. Oshigi was a family friend and my grandmother's next-door neighbor. She and her husband had taken Athena in as a foster child and raised her as their own. Once Mr. Oshigi passed away, Ms. Oshigi started taking in other children who had nowhere to go.

Today, she wore what she always wore on weekdays: a plain white buttoned-down shirt and jeans that she'd constantly mend and repair rather than buying a new pair. She was a fragile and petite woman with silvery-gray hair constantly tied into a bun. Her wrinkled skin had a yellowish undertone, and her deep brown eyes were full of wisdom.

With such a bittersweet reunion, Ms. Oshigi embraced me as soon as I stepped from the porch steps. "Finally, my love, your day has come," Ms. Oshigi said while hugging me with all her strength in her body.

"So you knew, too," I said softly.

"Everyone knew!"

"Everyone except us!" Miakoda called.

"Well, at least I'm not the only one," I replied while taking a few steps away from Ms. Oshigi.

I looked over at my friends who were trying their best to send me off tear-free. "It'll only be for two years, so it won't be like I'll be gone forever," I said, trying to minimize the situation, even though I was failing at it miserably.

"Two years is way too long! It's so going to be boring here without you, bestie," Anna exclaimed.

"You'll be missed," Rodney admitted calmly.

I made a sympathetic face. "How much time do I have left?" I asked, looking over at the ambassador who stood across from me.

"Thirty minutes. We need to get to the airport. Our flight will be leaving in one hour," she informed me.

Miakoda and Athena looked at each other as I made my way over to them. "Be sure to write and tell us all about Narea!" said Miakoda while giving me a hug.

Miakoda Smith was a petite girl with coper-toned skin who stood at only five feet three. She was a true country girl at heart; she enjoyed baking, eating Japanese barbecue, and American country music. Today, Miakoda looked the part, too, with her raven hair tied in a milkmaid braid. She wore a short denim romper, brown wedges with lace socks, and a sun hat adorned with a light pink ribbon shielding her dark-brown eyes.

I hugged my best friend tightly, but knowing that it was time, I let go of her. "I will, promise. I'll write to you every day."

Athena leaned against the tree that stood in front of my—well, what used to be my home. "You better! Otherwise, we're going to have some issues, Your Highness." We all had an outburst of giggles.

Athena de la Cruz was a tomboyish sporty girl who liked to spend most of her time on the girls' baseball team rather than in the school's orchestra. Unsurprisingly, she was the tallest of all of us, standing at five feet nine. The only reason Athena had joined the orchestra anyway was because of her demanding parents who'd rather see her onstage than on the field. She had short straight black hair, brown eyes, and a caramel tone to her skin.

"Yeah, okay, de la Cruz!"

"Miss Eleanor, it's time to go," Ms. Kim informed me.

"Coming," I replied while going over to pick up my suitcases. All my family, friends, and I exchanged our final glances as I got into the car and shut the door. Miakoda and Athena waved, standing adjacent to one another.

"Miakoda, Athena, see you!" I called from the car window.

"Take care," the two replied in unison.

"And don't forget about us little people!" Anna exclaimed while waving frantically.

I waved to my friends one more time, but this time, my eyes began to flood with tears. I slowly felt the car begin to move, gradually picking up speed. Once I got the chance to wipe my eyes, I watched everyone wave at me from the back window. When they faded out of sight, I turned to look out the window at the scenery passing by.

We soon made it to our small town, Crossroads. The local corner store, Larson's, was just starting to open for business along with the rest of the small shops and boutiques nearby. As we passed them, I tried looking at each storefront, seeing what each window display had to offer.

Once we reached the international airport, our driver dropped us directly in front of our jet. The flight crew lined up outside, greeting us warmly while taking both Kim's and my suitcases. Upon entering the custom-modeled private aircraft, I was blown away by its interior. Complete with a sleek sitting area with white leather seats, a large flat-screen television, a dining area, a full-sized bedroom, as well as a full-sized restroom, I felt like I was in an apartment in the sky!

During the duration of my twelve-hour flight, the ambassador educated me about the history of the Royal Family, the expectations of me as part of the royal line, and the school I would be attending starting in a few weeks.

Life as a royal sounded significantly more complicated than I'd initially thought. Having no public opinion regarding political matters, dressing modestly, and disabling my social media were just some of the practices I was expected to follow as Princess Royal, the title my father would bestow upon me. As the ambassador rambled on and on about my duties, I occasionally responded with slight nods, trying to keep up the rigid royal policies.

"Before the Great War of the East, it was tradition that royal children were to be homeschooled by a governess," explained Ms. Kim as we sat across from each other at the dinner table. "Unlike your father, you have the great opportunity to attend the Rosemary Windsor Academy. Your brother has been attending the Academy since kindergarten."

With the latter announcement, the fork in my hand fell to the floor with a clang. "Wait, I have a brother?!"

Before she could give an explanation, one of the attendants leaned in, whispering something inaudible. Her facial expression changing immediately to one of concern, she put down her fork and knife. "Excuse me, Young Miss, I'll be right back."

"Is something wrong?" I asked with sincere concern.

The ambassador stood up from her comfortable seat. "I'll explain later. For now, finish the rest of your food and try to get some rest. Tomorrow will be quite . . . busy."

With that, she took her leave, following the attendant to the staff quarters and shutting the sliding door behind them.

CHAPTER THREE

META

May 20, 2015

"Young Miss . . ."

"Young Miss . . ."

"YOUNG MISS!"

"AHH!" I yelled, quickly awakening from my slumber. After rubbing my eyes, I noticed Ms. Kim standing by my bed, peering down at me.

"Apologies for waking you so suddenly, but it's time to get you ready for landing."

I looked past her momentarily, staring out the window and into the darkness of the early morning. "Landing? Why do I have to prepare for that?"

"Last night, news broke out regarding your arrival in Narea, and the country is in an uproar. According to the palace's Public Relations Department, it's trending all over social media. Thus, it's highly likely that the news stations, as well as many others, will be present at the airport upon your arrival!" Ms. Kim's brows knitted together sympathetically. "Your father wanted to introduce you properly to the country himself, but unfortunately there have been some changes to our plan. Now that this is a public appearance, we should have you look well presentable."

Taking a seat on the small but comfortable vanity chair, I began to take in my disheveled appearance in the mirror. My naturally curly and frizzy hair was a tangled mess due to forgetting to pack my hair bonnet the day prior. Having just a baby-pink scrunchie, a boar-bristle hairbrush, and some E-Styler gel, I opted to slick my long mane back into a high ponytail that hung to my lower back as Ms. Kim watched in silence, intrigued. Digging into my makeup bag, I dabbed my caramel-toned concealer under my eyes, applied some skin tint, and pressed powder to my face, finishing my look with a shimmer gloss on my plump pink lips.

"So," I began while breaking the momentary silence, "you mentioned last night that I have an older brother?"

"Stepbrother," Ms. Kim corrected while taking a seat at the edge of my bed. "His name is Park Jung Hwa. Perhaps you're familiar with him and his mother?"

Park Jung Hwa . . . After trying to think of where I might have heard his name, some bells finally rang in my head. "He's the former prime minister's son, correct?" Silently, the Narean answered with a simple nod.

One of the world's men of means and eligible bachelors, Park Jung Hwa was the son of a nation's former prime minister and CEO of one of Narea's largest technology conglomerates. When his parents split a couple of years ago, the media outlets covered it for days, and the subject was the hot topic of conversation for many. Despite his parents being constantly in the limelight for their own personal reasons, little was known about Jung Hwa himself. He was a mystery living in the shadow of his parent's success.

Making a beeline to my suitcase, I quickly grabbed my favorite pair of bubblegum-pink sweats all for Ambassador Soo-Young to snatch my comfy, cozy outfit away from me.

"As I stated prior: as the daughter of the Emperor, you have to look presentable—meaning no sweats!" Opening the closet, she reached for a black garment bag revealing a buttoned knee-length forest-green-and-bronze sailor dress and brown Mary Janes. "In my opinion, this would be more fitting for the occasion, no?"

Glancing out the window at my new home, anxiety began to set in. Outside the plane was a sea of people already crowded in front of the large craft, phones ready in hand.

"Wow . . . so we're finally here," I muttered to myself.

"When you exit, there will be journalists that will try to bombard you with questions. Don't say anything; just stay close to the Royal Guards and me, and everything will be fine."

After taking a deep breath, the noise and anticipation from outside became louder as I followed the ambassador out of the aircraft and onto the soil of my new home.

Taking in the many faces of the strangers surrounding us, everything seemed to rush by like a blur as the guards rushed me over to a black Rolls-Royce, quickly ushering me off the landing mat and inside the small luxurious sedan. Ms. Kim briefly left me behind as she got to work addressing both the citizens and the press who had been anticipating our arrival. Out of sheer curiosity, I whipped out my phone to check the news.

Opinions were split. While some Nareans were welcoming, there was another part of the country—the vast majority, it seemed—who despised the fact that the king had procreated with a woman of non-Narean descent. My eyes scrolled through the various slurs and hate speech posted to the hashtag "*#PrincessLovechild.*"

After going back and forth with the media for a few moments, Ms. Kim took her place beside me. "It's probably best if you stay off of social media," she warned. "The media will often try to pry into your personal life now due to you being your father's daughter, and the paparazzi and journalists have already gained a reputation for being aggressive toward the royals and their associates."

"Anything for a story, huh?" I asked absentmindedly while I watched the crowd eventually disappear into obscurity as our car exited the airport.

"Precisely!"

Having had enough of the negativity and weightless assumptions online, I muted my notifications, tucking my phone away in my purse.

The distance between the airport and the palace was a good distance, about a thirty-minute trip with escort courtesy of the Narean Guard. As we passed the various landmarks of the capital, the ambassador passionately explained to me the historical significance of each one with pride. Various onlookers in other cars and on the street observed us with curiosity while our caravan comprised of security and local police passed them by, all attempting to get a glimpse of who was on the other side of the darkly tinted car windows.

Unification City lay within the heart of the country and sat on three former nations' borders who were once enemies. It is home to Parliament, the National Museum of Narea, and finally, the Chrysanthemum Palace—the place I would be calling home for the next two years of my life. Nicknamed the "Palace in the Heavens," the Chrysanthemum Palace proudly stood high on Unification Hill with its white stone and gold adornments. It's within the grand hall of this glorious structure where the founding fathers of this very nation signed the Treaty of Unity.

We reached the hilltop palace early in the evening during the sun's golden hour. Housemaids along with other palace employees formed a line from our car to the entrance of the palace. Despite being in awe of the beautiful structure that overlooked the view of the city, I did my best to compose myself as a handsome decorated guard of tall stature opened my door and assisted me out of the vehicle.

"Welcome home, Young Miss," the guard politely greeted. "I'm Qi Guowei. Your father has entrusted me to provide you with the utmost protection while here in our country."

"Nice to meet you! I entrust my safety to you." I held my hand out to Guowei, offering a polite handshake. However, he politely declined by taking two steps back, bowing slightly.

"I can assure you, you will be in good hands."

AFTER INSTRUCTING THE MAIDS TO BRING MY SUITCASES TO THE LIVing quarters, the stiff and stoic Guowei gave me a tour of the palace, with Ms. Kim trailing us and stopping our tour every so often to rattle off facts about the significance of a certain item displayed. With my expected arrival, no tours were being given to the public today. Stopping in the throne room, Guowei showed me a large brown book encased in glass. A thick velvet crimson rope surrounded the display, "No Photography" signs close by.

"Here before you now is the very treaty that started this nation," he said with reverence.

"The Unification Treaty of 1985," I whispered softly. Taking a step closer to the velvet rope, I saw the crisp signatures of the country's founding fathers. My father's name was scribbled in black ink on the signature line.

Along the way, I was introduced to some of the palace staff as well as other people who would be part of my day-to-day life here. There was the Palace Museum which was typically open to the public, the Royal Library that held all of the nation's significant documents, the servant quarters across the courtyard where some staff resided, the dining room, the formal living room, my father's office, and finally, the family's living quarters.

The third and fourth floors was where my family resided. This part of the palace was considered private quarters, only accessible to the Royal Family and trusted personnel. Guowei stopped in front of two white French doors with matching golden knobs.

"Young miss, your father had this room prepared for your stay," Ms. Kim said. Guowei opened the doors, revealing a large bedroom decorated in pink and white. The setting sun filtered in through the windows of the walkout balcony, creating small rainbow reflections from the crystal chandelier that hung above us. My white-and-pink velvet tufted bed was the centerpiece, adorned with a matching comforter set and a round black-and-white striped box of eternity roses. On the farthest wall to the left of my bed was a modest sitting area complete with a mounted flat-screen television situated in a gold frame above my dresser.

"Just so you know," said Soo-Young, "your father has been working on this room for the past year and a half. However, if there's anything not to your liking—"

"I love it!" I exclaimed. "When will I be able to thank him in person?"

"Your father is almost done with his last meeting for today. He'll be free afterward to meet with you," Guowei answered. "In the meantime, I'll leave Ambassador Kim to show you the rest of your room. I'll come to collect you when your father wraps up his business for today."

"Thanks for the tour, Guowei." I extended my hand again for a firm shake, head cocked to the side as my earth-hued eyes glanced up to meet his gaze. Before he could bow, I interjected, "You're not going to leave me hanging, are you?"

Guowei's dark-brown eyes looked down at my hand for a moment before meeting my eyes. "It's not customary to shake hands with you, Young Miss." He took two steps back. "It's considered proper to bow."

"Oh, I see . . ." I said a bit disappointedly. I mean, how else was I supposed to respond to that?

"Now, if you'll excuse me."

As soon as Guowei made his exit, Ms. Kim showed me the attached powder room and the large walk-in closet that already housed the clothes that had been neatly folded in my suitcase.

"You know, Guowei may be stoic and a stickler when it comes to rules . . . however, he means well," she explained while sitting adjacent to me on my white couch. I simply nodded silently. "While some of our customs here in Narea may be different from that of your home country, I'm sure with private etiquette and cultural lessons, in due time you'll begin to appreciate our way of life!"

Later that evening, Ambassador Kim and I parted ways for the night while Guowei led me to the dining room to meet my father. "Are you excited?" the young man questioned as we made our way down the stairs and into the main quarters of the palace.

Excited was an understatement, "Indeed I am! I have so many questions."

Guowei's long strides left me following a few steps behind him. I heard a deep and barely audible chuckle. "I'm sure you have plenty, Young Miss." At the end of the hall was the entrance of the dining room. "Typically, your family dines upstairs in the Royal Quarters. However, your father insisted we prepare the formal dining room for you tonight."

"How kind of him." Finally, just beyond the double wooden doors we faced, I was to meet the man whom I had been told for so many years was no longer on Earth.

My bodyguard raised a hand to the door handle and glanced down at me. "Are you ready, Young Miss?"

My brown eyes looked up to meet Guowei's gaze. I moved my head up and down like a bobblehead. "I'm ready."

With an assuring smile and a nod, he held open the door, allowing me to make my entrance. "Presenting Princess Eleanor Aurora Aladesanni Yamamoto, daughter of Abioye Aladesanni of the United States of America and His Royal Highness Emperor Yamamoto Hironori of Narea."

As I passed through the wide brown double doors, I took in the appearance of the man at the head of the table. The very face that had graced the pages of my school's history book was now before me. Emperor Yamamoto Hironori of Narea—who I'd soon be referring to affectionately as Father—was a well-respected man in high society. With tan skin, yellowish-brown eyes, and gelled raven-black hair parted to the left, his aura commanded respect.

A warm, welcoming smile lit up his face as the nearby butler directed me to the seat to the right of my father. Before he could pull back my seat, my father stood from his chair and embraced me in a warm hug. "Finally, after all these years, I can hug my daughter!"

This is like a dream! I deeply inhaled the scent of cigars coming off his clothes as I embraced my dad. "My family . . ." I informed him while tearing up slightly, "They said you were dead!"

He pulled away, staring into my glistening brown eyes. "Eleanor, I'm sorry, but I can explain." Gesturing for me to take a seat, I sat beside my father, awaiting his explanation for his lack of presence in my life growing up. "When I met your mother I was studying abroad at Howard."

"You chose to study at a historically Black university?" As an heir, surely there were many other options he could have pursued for his education.

"Yes, and I'm an alumnus. During my younger years, I was fascinated with Black culture and music. I grew up admiring it, so after high school, I decided to apply for a few HBCUs—of course, unbeknownst to my parents. They were indeed outraged once they found out," my father chuckled.

"While in America, I wanted to live a normal life, so I never told any of my friends about my bloodline and simply went by my childhood name, Hiro. Your mum was a freshman staying in the Greek village on campus at the time, and we met at a party that my friend's fraternity was hosting. She was an extraordinary woman—beautiful, book smart, adored the fine arts, and had a strong dislike of alcohol! She was unwillingly dragged along by her sorority sisters to let loose and sat idly on a lawn chair in the backyard, uncomfortably watching the madness unfold as her friends got wasted, red plastic cups in hand. I also was an unwilling participant, so your mum and I kept each other company that night. After that evening, we became very close, and eventually, our friendship turned into something more.

"I loved Abi dearly, as she fell for me when she didn't know of my wealth. We dated for two years, and we planned on getting married after she graduated. After graduating from Howard, I lost the desire to return to Narea, as I was content with my life in America. I had new aspirations and was ready to settle down and live a normal life with my fiancée. However, your grandparents weren't fond of this idea, especially when it came to marrying your mother. Then my father, the former emperor, became terminally ill before you were born, so as the next in line, I had to return to take his place.

"Abioye was in her last semester, and you were on the way. Before I left, we both made the joint decision to allow you to have the option of living a normal life or choosing to live the life I was accustomed to when you came of age. Growing up in a royal household was tough. The rules are quite strict, and I wasn't very fond of it as a child, so I wanted to give you a choice that I didn't have—to just be a kid."

With my food almost gone at this point, I adoringly listened to my father. "The week before I was scheduled to leave, your mum went into labor. It was a rainy Sunday night in early May. There was a downpour when I rushed your mother to the hospital. You were actually due in June, so it was a surprise to us both. Abioye struggled a lot when giving birth to you, and unfortunately, the complications were too much for her . . ."

"So she died," I whispered.

Despite the fact that this had all happened long ago, my father had a pained expression. "I'm sorry, Eleanor. That part of the story is true. After your mum died, I was heartbroken. I wanted to stay and raise you myself, but I knew I couldn't. So, I left you with your mum's sister, Carol. She was the most trustworthy individual I knew, and I knew she would uphold her sister's and my wishes to allow you to have a regular childhood."

After dinner, my father and I continued our conversation on the balcony that overlooked the courtyard of the palace. The sky was a midnight blue, with the lights of the city skyline and the vast clouds hiding the many stars that glimmered in the sky. The courtyard gardens below were quiet, and there was a gentle breeze that greeted us on occasion.

"So, how do you feel about all of this?" my father inquired.

"It's a lot to take in; it's somewhat exciting and overwhelming at the same time. Where do I even begin?"

My father's eyes shifted off me and out to the courtyard as a gust of wind greeted us once again. "It's understandable, Eleanor. I know so much has happened over the past few days. However, I'm confident you'll get the hang of it in due time. Soon, you'll begin your six-month training program where you'll learn the proper etiquette and protocol for how to be successful as a royal."

I glanced up at my father. "How soon?"

"Immediately, effective tomorrow morning. So, I suggest retiring early tonight to be well rested for your lessons."

We went back into the palace and Father walked me back to my room, bidding me a goodnight. "I'm sorry you were not able to meet your stepbrother and stepmum this evening. They had an engagement tonight in Helis and should be back sometime tomorrow morning."

"I'll be looking forward to meeting them. Thanks for dinner tonight—I really enjoyed it."

"No need to thank me. It was nice to have some one-on-one quality time. If Abioye was still here, she would've been so proud of you, Eleanor."

"Thanks, Dad. Well, I guess I'll get ready for tomorrow." Standing on my tippy-toes, I wrapped my arms around my father's tall frame, enveloping him in a warm hug. "Goodnight."

CHAPTER FOUR

MERIN

May 21, 2015

"So, here is today's agenda," Ms. Kim began. "After breakfast, you are to report to the study for your lessons, then you're free for the afternoon until dinner. Perhaps during this time you can do some exploring of the palace or visit the stables. Your aunt said you're fond of animals, especially horses."

This morning, the ambassador and I were enjoying breakfast on the balcony in my room, a modest plate of golden toast and eggs. "Stables?" I asked excitedly.

"Yes, located across the courtyard on the other side of the garden."

Looking through the vast swath of trees in all kinds of pinkish hues, I saw an old brown wooden structure of decent size. *Note to self: Visit the stable!*

After the morning meal, Ms. Kim walked me to the study. The halls outside the residential area were quite busy, with the ambassador and I passing many maids. Unfortunately, I didn't run into my father this morning. *Well, I'm sure he's a busy man.*

"Is the palace typically this busy?" I asked while giving a slight nod to a passerby.

"Not always. However, we are expecting your brother and stepmother today."

Oh, right! "Well, I look forward to meeting them tonight!"

"Here's the study. Your father's office is two doors down the hall, and my office is next door. I'll send your teacher in right away." With that, Ms. Kim and I said our goodbyes and parted for the time being.

I curiously headed inside the study. The room was decorated with a palette of pale green and gold trim, and forest-green and golden tassel drapes framed the large windows that let in the soft natural light. An oak desk was stationed not far from a wall full of books. Photos of some recognizable figures sporting emotionless expressions adorned the pale green walls, and one in particular garnered my attention. It captured a young boy in what appeared to be an equestrian uniform, proudly holding a rosette for first place. *Out of all the photos, he's the only one who's widely grinning.*

"Prince Jung Hwa when he was ten," an unfamiliar voice informed me, shifting my attention from the photo of my brother to a smartly dressed woman standing by the oak desk with a large book in her arms. "Ayotola. Feel free to call me Ayo," she said, setting down her book to clasp one of my hands with both of her own.

"Pleasure meeting you, Ayo. Are you my teacher?"

"Indeed I am, Young Miss! We'll be spending quite a bit of time together for the next few weeks."

Ayotola and I truthfully didn't spend much time on lessons; we mostly spent our time that morning getting to know one another.

Ayo had emigrated from the Kingdom of Helis to Narea as a naturalized citizen and was one of the most sought-after etiquette coaches in the nation. She stood at a modelesque height of five feet nine and had skin dark as ebony, deep-set brown eyes, and raven hair she secured in crown braids.

"So, looking over your school records, it appears that you have the habit of being tardy."

"Right . . . I guess you can say I'm mostly fashionably late," I deadpanned.

"Nice try, but we're going to work on that. Punctuality is an expectation, especially when it comes to the many activities that will become part of your daily life."

As Ayotola gave me an overview of my studies, I realized this program was quite extensive. Who knew Royal Academia consisted of everything from personal image to even courting etiquette?

As promised, after my morning lessons I was free to go exploring. It was a nice spring day out, and there were only a few people outside. Trying to remember Ms. Kim's directions by heart, I walked down the garden's pathway of cobblestone, following the sound of hooves marching. *Someone must be out there.*

Soon, I spotted what I was searching for. The stable held about a dozen horses, which were either asleep, minding their own business, or lightly neighing at me as I walked by. Each horse's name was engraved on a golden plaque above its stall. From where I stood, I could see Apollo, Dancer, Axel, and Ayasha. Only hay occupied Ayasha's stall at the moment.

Before moving on to the next stall, a horse across the way with hair and fur white as snow greeted me with a low neigh. "Hello, there," I said while striding calmly over to the white horse and reading its name plaque. "Winter!" The horse happily nickered, bobbing its head up and down.

"HEY!" boomed a shrill voice, startling both me and Winter. Prior to now, it had been only me and the horses in the stable. By Ayasha's stall stood a girl of average height dressed head to toe in riding gear. "Who are you, and what are you doing with the prince's horse?"

"The prince? The prince is my brother," I announced simply.

The copper-toned girl's eyes scanned me up and down. "Sure. Well, I'm sure you know palace policy. This is a private stable, meaning it's only available to the Royal Family and the Court. My father is the part of the latter, so I qualify."

Is this girl serious? She looked to be around my age, so I knew she couldn't hold any authority. Giving Winter a pat, I walked over to meet her. "Good for you, then. And who are you?"

"Priya Singh," the girl stated matter-of-factly. "Daughter of General Singh."

I eyed her up and down. "Humph, doesn't ring a bell. Pleasure meeting you. I'm Elle Yamamoto, daughter of Emperor Hironori Yamamoto."

"Hey, Priya, Ayasha's all good to go!" a male voice called from outside.

"I guess that's your cue to leave." I looked into her eyes unflinchingly.

"It was a pleasure meeting you, *Your Highness*," she scoffed. Priya walked past me, purposely bumping into my shoulder.

What an abrasive girl. Hopefully my stepmother and stepbrother will be more pleasant.

After spending a few more minutes at the Equestrian Center, I made my way back to the palace just in time to prepare for dinner. With the golden hour rays peeking through the French doors to my room's balcony, a black garment bag laid illuminated across my bed along with a white envelope with the family seal. As I ripped open the envelope, there was a knock at the door. "Come in," I called.

Suddenly a trio of girls entered the room, each carrying a plethora of beautification tools. Two of the three were petite and looked identical, while the other was tall and lean. "Hello, miss," said one while setting down her things. "I'm Everleigh, and these two are my younger sisters, Elena and Eden."

Both smaller girls bowed slightly in unison. "We're here to prepare you for this evening."

While the girls helped me look properly fancy for the evening ahead, we all chatted back and forth amongst each other. I learned Everleigh's and her sister's family, the Rosses, have been serving the Royal Family for over a decade. Their grandmother works in the kitchen, while their mum is the palace's seamstress.

"Elena, I must ask, are you and Eden twins?" I inquired while staring back at the two girls through my vanity mirror.

"Yep!" both girls answered in unison.

"I am the eldest, though," Eden announced.

"By two minutes," Everleigh added while putting brown bobby pins into the high bun she'd made on the crown of my head. "That should hold it! Have you taken a look at the dress yet?"

I glanced over at the black garment bag that sat between the twin girls on the bed. "Not yet."

Eden headed over to the vanity, holding up the garment bag. "Well, what are you waiting for? Open it!"

All the girls gathered around me. Unzipping it, I discovered a tea-length scarlet silk dress with spaghetti straps decorated with bows adorning each shoulder. "Wow, classy!" I gasped, admiring the garment's beauty.

"Pure class, indeed," Elena approved.

"And again, this is just for dinner?" I asked, holding the dress up to me.

"Just for tonight. You are meeting the Empress and the Prince this evening, after all," said Everleigh.

I twirled in my golden heels after getting changed, watching the round skirt of my dress sway in the mirror.

"Gosh, my mum makes a good dress!" exclaimed Eden.

"Your mum made this? Please give her my gratitude."

Not long after I was ready, Guowei came to escort me to the dining room. "You look stunning tonight," he complimented, taking my arm in his. "How was last night?"

"Went better than I imagined. The one-on-one time was pretty nice."

"I am glad things went smoothly. Empress Angeline and Prince Jung Hwa have returned this afternoon, so they'll be joining you and your father this evening."

I hummed, already aware of the fact. "Tell me, what are they like, Guowei?"

He stayed silent for a beat, with only the sounds of our footsteps audible as we walked to the dining room. "I have had too few interactions with your brother to really form an opinion. As for your stepmother, she is rather . . . interesting."

"I see . . ." Noticing Guowei's reluctance to discuss my family, I decided to change the subject. Once we were in front of the large French doors leading into the dining room, he quickly wished me well as we parted ways.

The table was set immaculately with white fine china and crystal glasses that glimmered and reflected light from the chandelier from above. Alone in the massive room I sat, finding the napkin in my lap quite interesting as I nervously waited for my family to show.

A faint clicking of stilettos against the marble floor echoed from the other side of the door. *Someone's coming.*

"Introducing Her Highness Empress Angeline of Narea," a man announced, opening the door to reveal a beautiful, smartly dressed middle-aged woman of average stature. She had a powerful presence, somehow commanding all of your attention as she glided through the room.

Being the only other person present, I stood as she approached. "Good evening," I warmly greeted her.

"Evening," she said simply.

"It's a pleasure to finally meet you. How was your trip?" I asked while we both took our seats.

"Fine," she stated flatly. "Listen, enough with the pleasantries. Since it's only us ladies at the moment, allow me to make this crystal clear: You are a stain on my family, and you are not welcome here. At best, you are only a temporary tenant in this residence. I will never accept a mutt as my daughter."

"A mutt? Really? I was just trying to be polite. I may not be your daughter, but I am my father's, and he said I get to choose my path. I'll be here for a long, long, *long* time, so for the sake of my dad and the peace of this household, let's play nice."

A witchy stepmother. Brilliant! We both sat in tense silence across from each other as we waited for my stepbrother and father. Despite my attempt to break the ice with my stepmom, she only replied with curt answers. *Don't want to talk? Fine, I'll just message my friends.*

To escape the awkward tension, I looked down at my phone screen, deciding to vent to Anna. *So how are you liking palace life so far?* she asked.

E: . . . Alright, I guess.

A: Alright? Girl, you're literally living the high life, you lucky duck! Is your dad a royal pain or something?

E: Okay, first off, it's only been one day, and two, Dad seems pretty chill so far. It's just some of the people here that are—

"Are what?" asked an unfamiliar male voice. Looking over my shoulder, a tall dark-haired man with matching almond-shaped eyes was staring down at me and my phone.

I was so busy texting away, that I hadn't even realized another person had entered the dining room. I'd only seen blurry, grainy photos of this man briefly in teen magazines and tabloids back home, and the photos did not do him justice. *He's handsome.*

"Thanks, and you look nice, too," he chuckled, plopping down in the seat adjacent to me.

"Did I just say that out loud?"

"Yes. Yes, you did."

My face grew hot in embarrassment, my cheeks becoming a rosy hue. *Yikes, way to go, Elle.* "Sorry. Jung Hwa?"

"Yep! You're Elle, right? Dad told me a lot about you."

"Hopefully good things?"

Despite the rough start, dinner went smoothly. While I obviously wasn't Angeline's favorite person in the world, she at least tolerated my presence. As soon as Dad joined us, she plastered on the fakest smile I'd ever seen, carrying on about her visit to the Kingdom of Helis to my father as he listened intently. The interaction between us was limited, with her wide grin never meeting her eyes. It was so easy to see right through her. As for Jung Hwa, he was a breath of fresh air. After lessons tomorrow, he promised to meet me at the Equestrian Center.

When I had retired to my room afterward, Elena asked, "So, how did it go?" while brushing my hair. Eleanor and her sisters had my nightdress set out on my bed, along with a pair of house slippers. I sat at the edge of my bed in my pajamas while Elena brushed my locks and the other two gathered around me, listening intently as I ranted on about my frustrations.

"First off, the empress!" I said, throwing my arms up.

All the girls sighed in unison. "Yeah, she's horrid, isn't she? Not the most tolerant," said Eden.

"I can't stand her!" Elena exclaimed.

"All of this is very different from what I'm used to. I was hoping to have at least a decent relationship with my stepmother, but I guess that's not happening anytime soon," I sighed.

"Hey, don't take it personally," said Everleigh. "I can assure you, she's the most difficult person here. Trust me, before you arrived, my sisters and I had to take care of her."

"Mmhmm, she's a royal pain in the—"

"Eden!" Everleigh interrupted, giving her younger sister a disapproving look.

"What? It's true!" Our giggles filled the room. "Well, hopefully tomorrow will be a better day."

I really hope so.

CHAPTER FIVE

MÁÀRÚN

May 28, 2015

Instead of having breakfast on the terrace, Dad wished for us to begin our day in the dining room. Days started early in the palace, with my personal assistants waking me at seven o'clock in the morning. Unfortunately, I had never been a morning person. Whenever I had to wake up early, I felt like an old computer trying to start up.

Everleigh forced open the curtains to the terrace, allowing the sun's radiant light to illuminate the room. "Gooood morning, Elle!" she chirped.

Wake-up sequence is activated. Loading . . . 5 percent. I reluctantly peeled open my eyes. *10 percent.* I let loose a yawn while stretching my limbs. "Morning, Everleigh," I greeted groggily. *30 percent.* "Where's Elena and Eden?"

"Helping our nan. They're short-staffed in the kitchen this morning, so they're assisting with breakfast." Once I finally rose from the bed, Everleigh assisted me in getting ready, laying out a lovely riding outfit for me and slicking my hair into a low ponytail.

"So, what does my schedule look like for today?" I asked as we both headed to the dining room.

Whipping out a smartphone, she read out my plans for the day. After breakfast I would have lessons with Ayo, and then Jung Hwa and I would go riding! But there was one other thing. Dad and I were supposed to have a meeting later this afternoon to go over some things. What "things," I wasn't so sure.

Dad was the only one in the dining room besides the servants setting the table and bringing out our food. "Good morning, Elle!" he called.

"Morning, Dad!" After embracing my father, I took a seat across from him.

"How are your lessons?" he inquired.

"They're going well. Ayotola and the others have been welcoming."

"I'm glad you're adjusting well. I'm sure you noticed something extra on your schedule?"

"Yes, our meeting. About that—"

"Morning, Elle!~," my brother said cheerily, making his way to the table. Today he was dressed smartly in what appeared to be a school uniform.

"Morning, Jung," I greeted as he sat adjacent to me.

Shortly after my stepmom joined us, we proceeded to eat. Breakfast was fairly light, but filling. We indulged our appetites while making casual conversation with one another. So far, things between Angeline and I were surprisingly cordial this morning. While she was still cold as ice, she still engaged with me a bit. As a newcomer, the last thing I wanted was unnecessary drama, so hopefully, there would continue to be peace between us. For Dad's sake.

"So, we're still on for this afternoon?" I asked.

"You know it, kid," Jung said, patting my head.

"What's planned this afternoon?" Angeline asked.

"Going to show little sis around the Equestrian Center, Mum."

"Ah, have fun," she replied flatly.

As soon as he finished, Jung bid us a good day, taking his leave. "Dear, remember we have a meeting with General Singh in a few minutes," Angeline then reminded Dad.

"Go ahead and greet the general for me. I'll be down in a few."

"As you wish. See you soon." Crossing her utensils across her plate, Angeline got up from her seat and strode out of the dining room.

"Back to what we were discussing earlier. There are a few things I wish to discuss with you regarding your role as a working royal. Now that you're settled in, I think it's imperative that we start including you in affairs."

"So soon? I just started my lessons! I still don't know much of anything regarding protocol—"

"I'm sure you'll be fine. The sooner, the better," my father confirmed, holding my hand in his. "Each one of us has a purpose here, and your purpose, Eleanor, is very special."

With breakfast finished, Dad left for his meeting while I headed to the classroom. Ayo was already there waiting for me.

"Dress and grooming," she started. "Regardless of where you are or what you do, you are first and foremost a member of the Royal Family. As the daughter of the emperor, you're expected to be a good example for girls and young ladies nationwide, but most importantly, to carry yourself with grace and elegance." Today's lesson focused solely on grooming, and goodness were the regulations overwhelming. Some of the rules about what could and couldn't be worn eliminated basically fifty percent of my wardrobe.

All dresses or skirts must be no shorter than above the knee, sheer stockings must be worn when not wearing pants, no blue denim whatsoever, hair must be done at all times, nails can be painted pale pink or nude only, makeup cannot too heavy . . . it never ends.

"Don't you think this is a bit much, Ayo?" I asked while observing some example outfits on three mannequins in front of me. Ayo had each dressed for different occasions. The last mannequin wore a gray and black gold-threaded plaid jumper skirt with a long white balloon-sleeve blouse. A bow was neatly tied around the collar, and an embroidered golden crest was on the left side of the chest. *Must be my school uniform.*

"Hmm, I think it's fairly reasonable compared to some other Royal Families' grooming policies. It may be a bit of an adjustment for you, but trust me, the rules are in place for a reason. It's just more conservative and modest, yes, but still stylish. Classics never go out of style."

I also learned that tomorrow, for the very first time, I would be heading into town with Ayo for a color analysis appointment. According to her, it was designed to help determine which colors look flattering on me and would complement me best.

After my lesson, as promised, Jung Hwa met me at the Equestrian Center. "Hey, Jung!" I called as I entered the stables. Winter immediately welcomed me with a friendly neigh from her stall.

"Hey, sis."

"How was your day?" I asked.

"Eventful. Had a pretty full schedule. How were your lessons?"

"They were fine, just went over the dress policy. I am definitely going to have to make adjustments," I lamented, giving Winter a head pat.

"One of the many fun things about being a royal," Jung said sarcastically.

"Totally. So, a little birdie told me that you're an equestrian expert . . ."

"I wouldn't say an *expert*," he replied modestly, "but Winter and I have been together for a long time. You ride?"

"It's been a while. My aunt and I lived in the suburbs, so we didn't have enough room for a horse. Last time I went riding was back in summer camp in '08." A smile grew on my face as I briefly mentioned the fond memory. "My knowledge is pretty rusty!"

"If you're interested, I wouldn't mind training you. I'm part of the university's Equestrian Team."

"That'd be awesome!"

And so my older bro and I spent the remainder of our free time together, exchanging various stories of our different upbringings. Jung had moved into the palace at an early age and fully embraced his role as a royal. After his mum's and dad's separation, which had been widely publicized, he enjoyed a comfortable, semiprivate life away from the spotlight and mostly found joy in horseback riding, gaming, and traveling. He was quite the extrovert, well loved by his many friends acquired through school and his past journeys.

"Any other interesting plans for this week?" I quipped as we both sat by a nearby bench.

"Aside from a meeting this Saturday, nothing much else. What time are you supposed to meet with Dad again?"

Taking a quick glance at my phone, I shot up from my seat. "In ten minutes!" I had been enjoying Jung's company so much, I had completely lost track of time.

"You better get going! You still can make it if you run."

"I hope so—I had so much fun today! See you around!" I said hurriedly, making a run for it. One of my worst habits was being tardy. *If I'm late, I'm positive I'll receive an earful from Ayo tomorrow, and possibly from Dad too.*

Following the directions a maid gave me, I reached the office just in time. I knocked on the door first, announcing my arrival. The door swung open, putting me face-to-face with a middle-aged man adorned in a military uniform. He had a brown complexion, slightly lighter than mine, and his hair was hidden under a matching forest-green turban. His stature towered above my measly average height of five feet seven.

I looked up at the well-decorated giant. "Oh, I'm sorry, I must be in the wrong place. I'm supposed to meet my father at his office."

"Oh, you must be the emperor's daughter. No, you're in the right place." The tall man stepped aside, allowing me to enter the moderately sized office. There my father sat behind a wooden desk, his attention occupied by a packet of documents.

"Hey, Dad," I greeted.

My father looked up, meeting my gaze. "Elle, right on time!"

I looked between the two gentlemen. "Am I interrupting something?"

"Not at all, we were just wrapping up," the unnamed man assured me.

My father stood from his desk to approach us. "Eleanor, this is General Singh, head of our Department of Defense."

"Pleasure meeting you, General."

"The pleasure is all mine," said Singh. "All arrangements will be in place for next month, Your Highness."

"Wonderful, we'll discuss further plans later this week. Thank you, General Singh!" After a brief farewell, the general left me and my father alone. Dad motioned for me to take a seat across from him.

"So how was your day?" I asked.

"Quite productive. The general and I were making security preparations for an upcoming engagement next month."

"The formal?"

"Yes—ah, Jung must have told you. We hold it every year for charity. This year, however, will be particularly special, as it's also doubling as your introduction to society," my father stated proudly.

"Wow, already? I just recently started classes, and I still have ways to go according to Ayotola."

"Like I stated earlier, the sooner, the better. Nareans, like most people, are very curious, so it's best that we give you a formal introduction before the media starts jumping to conclusions and spinning their own narrative."

CHAPTER SIX

MÉFA

May 29, 2015

At high noon, the streets of Unification City were full of life! In awe, I watched the many men, women, and children going about their business from the tinted window of a black sedan. Ayo sat beside me, going over the day's agenda, but her voice faded into the background as my eyes stayed glued to the bustling city just outside. *A city which I plan on exploring.*

"Got it?" Ayo asked after glancing up from her phone. I absent-mindedly parroted my schedule back to her. "Great!"

"Ayo, after running errands today, could we stay out a bit? Since coming here, I've never been outside the palace."

"I suppose we can. Guowei would be a great tour guide. He's a native!"

Hearing his name, Guowei's eyes glanced in the rearview mirror at us. "Sounds like a plan," he agreed.

Our car came to a halt in front of a modest-looking red brick building with a nicely decorated storefront. "*Wescott Image Consulting,*" I read out loud.

"This is the place. Brenda does amazing work. She's done image consultations for many people in high society," she informed me. Ayo took a look at her phone. "She's ready. Let's go."

Ayo and I headed inside, while Guowei stood guard outside. An average-sized woman with a milky complexion greeted Ayo with a hug. "Great to see you again, Ayotola. It's been a while," she said in an accent I attempted to match a country to.

"It certainly has," Ayo chirped. "This is my student."

"Ms. Yamamoto, it's a pleasure to meet you," she greeted.

"Likewise," I said politely.

Brenda motioned us into her office, sitting me down as she went to grab fabric swatches in various hues. Ayo watched on as Brenda proceeded to hold different-colored fabrics up to my face and make her assessments. She repeated this action countless times, stopping every once in a while to jot down some notes on a sheet of paper. "So, Miss Yamamoto, you have a warm yellow undertone, which means the colors that will compliment you best are autumn and winter, respectively!"

"Seasons?" I asked, puzzled.

"Yes, seasons represent a color family. The later the season, the warmer and bolder the colors," Ayo explained.

"Exactly. While we may all have a favorite go-to color, it's still nice to be cognizant of what palette highlights and flatters you best," Brenda added. "As for metals, gold would make a bolder statement on you compared to silver."

"Indeed, it would," Ayo agreed. "So now that we know your palette, I'll send your file over to the family stylist so she can get to work."

Once we wrapped up at Brenda's, Ayo and I said our goodbyes and headed back to the car. "Young miss, do you have any particular place in mind?" asked Guowei, glancing back at us in the back seat.

It was now after three, and the last time we'd eaten was early this morning. "I would appreciate a decent meal."

Guowei hummed in agreement. "There's the Diamond Box Cafe not far from here. It's really cute," Ayo suggested.

"Cute, yeah—food quality, however, not so great. If I'm going to give Young Miss a tour, we're going to do this right. No touristy stuff," declared Guowei.

"Fine," Ayo said, "no touristy stuff. There's a nice restaurant I often frequent that's pretty nice. It's nothing fancy, but the couple that owns the place makes a great okonomiyaki."

"Mmm, sounds good to me!" I beamed.

The afternoon in the city was a much-needed break from the regimental life at the palace. For the first time, I was able to let my guard down and enjoy Unification City as a tourist. Guowei, Ayo, and I had a late lunch at a small family-owned okonomiyaki shop nestled in a fairly quiet part of town on a backstreet. Luckily, we didn't draw too much attention, as the sweet old shopkeeper sat us in the back of her modest restaurant. Afterward, Guowei gave us a mini tour of the city, proudly showing me some of the places he frequented. Ayo, on the other hand, took us to a local market.

Since coming here, I've had to make so many adjustments; I always feel on edge as I try to live up to everyone's standards. With school vastly approaching and the Charity Ball only weeks away, I knew I still had a ways to go.

When we finally returned to the palace, it was dusk. Ayo turned in for the night, leaving me and Guowei outside my family's living quarters. "So, tomorrow's Saturday. Any fun plans for the weekend?" I asked him while walking down the hall to my room. Guowei followed behind, carrying my shopping bags full of trinkets and small souvenirs from our outing.

"Me? I'm on the clock tomorrow."

"You have to babysit me even on weekends, Guowei? You deserve some time off." My first impression of Guowei had been that he was stiff and boring, but hanging out with him today had shown me a more fun, outgoing side that was previously hidden. It was truly day and night like I was with a totally different person! "Thanks for today. You have no idea how much I needed that little break."

As we entered my room, Guowei placed the bags in my closet. "It was my pleasure. I know a lot of this stuff can be overwhelming. Sometimes it's good to step away every once in a while."

"Amen to that," I agreed while kicking my shoes off.

Guowei made his way to my bedroom doors. Before taking his leave, he turned to me, offering a word of reassurance. "If you ever feel overwhelmed or need to vent, I am willing to listen."

"Thanks, I'll keep that in mind. Goodnight, Mr. Qi."

"Goodnight, Young Miss."

After our late lunch, my stomach was still satisfied. I peeled out of my posh attire and settled into a plain white nightgown. As I went to grab my trusty silk scarf and brush to wrap my hair, my aunt's name flashed across my phone screen. Sitting down at my vanity, I pressed the Answer button and propped my phone up against my mirror.

"Hey, Elle!" she beamed.

"Hey, Auntie, how are things?"

"I've been well, just busy at the office as usual. I swear, that place has become my home away from home!"

My aunt and I rambled on for hours, catching up with the latest events in one another's lives. Before I knew it, it was already close to midnight. After saying our goodbyes, I plugged in my phone, placed it on top of my nightstand, and allowed sleep to consume me.

Brilliant rays of sunlight peeked through the curtains to my bedroom the next morning. Awaking me from my slumber, I stretched my arms to the ceiling, releasing a barely audible yawn. Correction: the curtains were wide open. *Last time I checked, they were closed . . .*

"Ah, the princess is finally awake," said a familiar voice. Slightly startled, my eyes cut over to my left. There sat Guowei, who had pulled my vanity chair over to sit by my bed.

"Guowei! Goodness, you scared me!" I exclaimed. "What time is it?"

He looked down at his phone. "About one in the afternoon."

Gosh, I overslept! "Oh no . . . Dad is probably worried that I didn't show up for breakfast."

"Your Highness is fine," Guowei assured me. "He had some business to attend to this morning, so you have nothing to worry about."

"How long have you been here?" I inquired. Pushing the plush duvet off my body, I sat up, throwing my legs over the edge of my mattress.

"Since this morning," answered Guowei.

For that long? He didn't look preoccupied with anything. I hummed in response. "Yet you didn't bother to wake me. You must have been bored."

"Actually, you're quite entertaining when you're asleep, Young Miss."

My cheeks turned rosy at this revelation. "Guowei!" I immediately sprung up from the bed and closed the distance between us, slapping him in the face.

Guowei held his stinging cheek, which was quickly turning red, mumbling words in another language I couldn't comprehend. "Ouch," he whined. "You move around a lot and talk in your sleep!"

"Lies!" I hissed.

"It's true!" he exclaimed while holding his hands up in defense. "Trust me, I wouldn't make this up. Next time I'll record you so you can see yourself."

Dropping the subject, I headed over to my closet and pulled out a simple white maxi dress. "So, what are the plans for today?" I asked, placing my completed coordinates on my bed.

"Hmm, we're in the clear. What are you in the mood for?"

"To have a little fun!" I announced. "You're the designated tour guide. What's fun to do around here?"

Guowei shrugged. "Depends on what you're into. What do you normally do for fun?"

"I like music," I began.

"You like music," he repeated flatly.

"No, *love* it! Regardless of the genre, as long as it's good, I'll give it a chance. Back in my home country, my friends and I would attend concerts and festivals together."

Guowei listened intently as I rambled on passionately. "So if you had to choose one genre to listen to, what would it be?"

"Hmm . . . such a difficult decision." My eyes moved toward the ceiling in thought. "Going by my Musify favorites playlist alone, the majority is either K-pop, hard rock, or metal."

Guowei's eyes widened in shock at the latter. "Rock and metal? Never would have guessed, Young Miss!"

"Yeah," I chuckled, "I get that a lot. I love rock. Nothing like a good headbanger to jam out to."

With that, Guowei got up from his seat and headed toward the door. "Noted. Why don't you go ahead and get dressed? Once you are finished, meet me downstairs."

"Okey dokey," I beamed. "Where are we going?"

The man smirked. "That's for me to know, and for you to find out. Get ready!" With that, he exited my quarters, shutting the door behind him to allow me privacy.

Once fully dressed, I went down to meet Guowei. I decided on an empire waist white halter maxi dress that barely hit the floor, cork wedges, and a gold-foiled leaf headband that adorned my crown. My hair flowed down my back, as today I was allowing it to hang freely. "Alright, ready," I said as I made my way down the stairway, the cork wedges clicking against the marble floor announcing my arrival. Guowei sat in the formal living room, one leg crossed over his knee. His attention was on the illuminated screen of his phone.

"Alright, let's get going." Together, we exited the palace and headed to the car.

Our destination was still a big mystery to me. Sitting in the back of the sedan, I chatted with Guowei through the partition, both of us engaged in a friendly debate on different various music artists. "What bands do you listen to primarily?" he inquired.

"The bands I listen to are pretty old," I began. Going through my playlist, I proceeded to list off various band names.

"Wow, you actually have good taste," he answered.

"Duh!" I shot back. Classics never got old. Friends back at home would go as far as calling me a music snob. I was super passionate about my tunes.

In a pleasant turn of events, Guowei took me to a music shop right outside the city. It was a modest suburb, and apparently he frequented the place often. The storefront was impressively decorated and displayed vintage memorabilia. After parking our ride, I excitedly got out of the vehicle before Guowei could make it to my door.

Upon entering, I was greeted with the aroma of gently used vintage vinyl and rows of albums. Noticing the obnoxious display for SHINee's newest single, I made a beeline to the special edition CD. "You're a fan of these guys?" asked Guowei.

"*Love* them!" I exclaimed passionately. We had apparently come during a slow time, as there weren't many customers browsing the store. There was a single worker on shift, who was chummy with Guowei. They greeted each other with a bro hug.

The employee's manner of dress was relaxed, sporting an oversized band tee, black skinny jeans, and Chucks. He was a tad shorter in stature from Guowei.

"Young Miss, this is Arlo," Guowei introduced us.

"Hey," Arlo greeted casually. I learned Arlo was Guowei's cousin, and this shop was owned by his family. After shooting the breeze, Guowei took me downstairs into a dark room. When he switched on the light, the space was revealed to be a music room. There was an electric guitar displayed on the wall, along with a bass. A red drum kit sat neatly in the corner.

"Guowei," I began, "this is amazing! Do you play?"

Instead of a verbal answer, he grabbed the guitar from the wall, plugging it into the amp, and proceeded to shred. "Okay, I'll take that as a yes."

"You play?" he asked, taking a seat in one nearby chair.

I shook my head. "I wish."

"Well, it's never too late. Sit down." He motioned for me to take a seat beside him. He placed the guitar in my lap and handed me a small pick. For the remainder of the afternoon, he gave me a mini lesson. As a lefty, I struggled to grasp a few things, but by the end of our session I could actually play a few chords!

Coming up from the basement, the streetlights were on and the sky was pitch-black. "That was so much fun! Can we come back another time?" I asked Guowei.

"Of course," said Arlo. "You'll always be welcomed. A friend of my cousin is a friend of mine. Plus, you should come see us play! Guowei is the guitarist for our band."

"You're in a *band?* I'd love to see you play!" I quipped, turning to Guowei.

"Yeah, we're just a cover band. We mostly play a ton of Type O songs and occasionally music from HIM."

"Some of my favorites!"

"Seriously?" both guys said in unison.

"Yeah! I have a few Type O posters in my room back in Cali."

"Would've never guessed," Arlo said with intrigue. "We have a pretty cool princess. You got my seal of approval!"

“Thanks,” I giggled. After saying our goodbyes to Arlo, we headed back to the palace.

Chapter Seven

Meje

June 1, 2015

It was finally the fated Monday—my first day at the Academy. This would be my first time ever starting mid-semester, so I wasn't sure how well I would be received. I was just hoping and praying I would have a decent class. Unlike American schools, students here stayed in one class while the teachers switched rooms throughout the day.

First days are always nerve-racking, but luckily I had Jung Hwa. Dad and Angeline were in a meeting already, so us two were left to our own devices. With my dark-brown locks secured in twin tails, donning my immaculate uniform, I headed down to the dining room to grab a quick bite to eat before heading out. A fairly modest breakfast sat on the table: golden toast, egg whites, and avocado. After chasing my breakfast down with some orange juice, I left the family living quarters to meet my brother outside.

The sun had barely revealed itself, and the morning dew was still present on the lush grass. Guowei greeted me properly, like always, and helped me into the car. "Morning, Jung!"

My brother sat adjacent to me, currently focused on a tablet. He peered up from the blue-lit screen illuminating his face. "Hey."

Rosemary Windsor Academy was located outside the city. The four-hundred-acre campus boasted picturesque views of the countryside and looked over a sparkling lake. The school housed students ranging from primary school to university, with each part of the campus separated by three buildings. Protected by gates of onyx iron, its student body was composed of the sons and daughters of the country's elite. In front of the gates was a line of numerous cars, each dropping off students of all ages.

"So you're in your last year, right?" my brother inquired.

"Yep!" I answered by popping the *P*.

"Okay, so you'll be in the main building. The headmaster's office is located there as well. We're going to have to stop by there to get your supplies and class information."

Once our sedan reached the main entrance, we parted ways with Guowei and headed down the tree-lined cobblestone path. There was a lively sea of youth wearing the uniforms of their respective levels, and the main path fed into a large quad, I could see each of the main buildings. The high school sat in the center and had a large bell tower.

Once we made it to the front office, my brother left to head to his own class and I headed inside. A heavyset secretary was typing away at her desk. Busy with her assignment, she paid me no mind as I stood before her, backpack slung over my shoulder. "Excuse me," I began, attempting to get her attention. "Today's my first day, and I was told to pick up my schedule."

The woman peered at me over her Coke bottle glasses. "Name?" Once I gave her all the information she inquired, she reached into her gray file cabinet, pulled out a few sheets of paper, and slapped down the stack in front of me. "Alright, Ms. Yamamoto, here's both your syllabus, classroom number, and locker information. Just sit tight, and your class leader will be by soon to take you to class."

Sitting outside the office on one of the available benches, I watched my new classmates shuffle through the halls. "Elle?" said a familiar voice.

A feeling of relief washed over me when I was met with a familiar face. "Arlo? I didn't know you went here!"

"Yeah, your father got me in here. Due to Guowei working at the palace and all . . ." Unlike his relaxed appearance the other day, Arlo was dressed smartly in the Academy's attire, his bag slung over his shoulder.

"So, what brings you to the headmaster's office?"

"I'm supposed to meet a new student."

I popped up from my seat and grabbed my bag. "Ah, yes, that would be me!" I allowed Arlo to lead the way as we weaved through the halls of the building. Large windows lined the walls, allowing passersby to peek into each classroom. Golden plaques sat adjacent to the sliding doors, identifying each room with its designated number.

We stopped in front of a slightly open door—room 2-A. "Here's our class." Opening the door and stepping to the side, Arlo allowed me to enter first. Class had yet to begin, and the students were too busy chatting amongst one another to pay me any mind. Letting out a loud whistle, the class grew silent as Arlo entered the room. Everyone's attention was drawn to us immediately as we stood in front of the room.

"Good morning, 2-A. We have a new student that'll be joining us for the remainder of the year."

As he gestured to me, I waved shyly. Whispers began to erupt throughout the space. Ignoring the murmuring, I briefly introduced myself. "Hey, I'm Elle. I'm originally from California, and now I call Unification City home."

"Let's all welcome Elle to our class," Arlo encouraged. A few students shouted "Welcome!" while others continued to murmur to each other. A group of girls in the back by the window were huddled around one particular girl's desk, looking at something on her phone. So far, my reception felt lukewarm.

"Are seats assigned here?" I asked, turning to Arlo.

"Not really, but the majority of us are creatures of habit. You can take any open desk."

Doing a quick scan of the area, I found a couple of options with vacancy: one in front of the girls gossiping by the window, the other in front of the teacher's desk. Picking my poison, I settled into the desk nearest to me.

Suddenly, there was a ruckus in the hall. Everyone's attention turned to the window, witnessing all the action—a scuffle between two girls. One was on the floor with her school books and other belongings scattered all around her. Her face showed utter fear, tears brimming in her hazel eyes. Her uniform looked slightly different, a jumper skirt reaching just past her ankles, and her hair was tucked into a silky baby blue hijab. The other girl towered over her with a smirk on her face. *She looks quite familiar . . .*

"Priya, please—" the girl on the ground pleaded.

"I gave you *one task,* yet you couldn't even do that!" With a swift kick, Priya knocked the defenseless girl on her back. The young hijabi groaned in agony. "All you had to do was obey, and do what I wanted! It's not rocket science, Farah."

"It's against the school's code of conduct! Eventually, the professor would've found out," Farah defended, albeit still shivering with fear. "Then we'd both be suspended!"

"Well thanks to your moral code, now *I'm* going to have to pay the consequences."

Just as Priya grabbed Farah by the shirt, the two girls were separated by a female teacher. "Enough!" the woman bellowed, directing her anger toward Priya. At this point, the whole class was crowded in front of the window, phones out and recording the victim's despair. Not one student intervened to defend Farah. Perhaps I would've been braver and stood up for her if it hadn't been my first day.

The woman who swooped into the rescue, I learned, was Ms. Honda, my homeroom teacher. She was a slightly chubby lady of average stature with a pale complexion. After checking on Farah, she sent Priya to the front office. "Rosemary Windsor's policies are clear," Ms. Honda began. "Bullying is strictly prohibited and will not be tolerated."

Releasing a large sigh, Ms. Honda entered the room and headed to her desk. "Please be seated." Everyone returned to their seats with no trouble. "If any posts or videos of this are discovered online, I promise the owner of those accounts will have special spots reserved for them in detention. Courtesy of the headmaster himself."

Despite the rough start, the rest of 2-A's morning went pretty smoothly. Soon, I had finished my first rounds of modern literature, Narean history, and politics lessons. When it came time for lunch, two students assigned to lunch duty bought in a couple of carts. All of us queued up single file, with myself behind Arlo. "Any plans for lunch?" I inquired.

"Yes, actually," said Arlo. "I have a meeting with the Student Council. We meet once a month."

"Oh, okay . . ."

"Sorry, Elle." Stepping up to a metal cart, we were both handed a metal tray complete with a plate of curry rice, soup, and a bottle of milk. "How about we get together for lunch tomorrow?"

I kindly accepted Arlo's offer with a smile and a nod. "So I'm assuming everyone just chills here for lunch period?"

"Most do, but I typically like getting some fresh air. On the roof of the building, there's a small garden run by the garden club here. The view is decent up there, so I go often."

Looking back at my classmates, I debated internally whether I wanted to eat at my desk or go to the roof. Apart from Guowei's cousin, I'd had very little interaction with the rest of my peers. After a couple of failed earlier attempts to start conversations with my desk neighbors, I decided to stick to myself for the rest of the morning. Even when we had to pair up for math, everyone seemed to already have arrangements.

Choosing to get some fresh air, I took my phone along with my tray and allowed Arlo to show me the way. The sun shone warmly in from the courtyard, illuminating the mostly empty hallways, as some classes were still in session. Arlo identified some of the rooms as we passed. A few doors down from 2-A was the science lab, and adjacent to that was the music room. Once we reached the stairwell, we said our goodbyes and went our separate ways.

Following his directions, I went up two flights of stairs until I reached two double doors. Greeted by a gust of wind, I took in my surroundings. It was a little after one and the skies were clear as crystal. The sun hung high in the sky, emitting its brilliant rays. There were numerous stacks of fresh vegetables lining the farthest wall along with flowers of various hues. Benches lined the adjacent wall, where students could look out and get a bird's-eye view of the Academy's track and soccer field.

Besides myself, there was only one other student. She sat alone on the last wooden bench, watching the tiny specks below running drills on the soccer field. As I got closer, I recognized her as the girl from earlier. She rested her head on the palm of her hand, her rhinestone barrettes clipped to each side of her baby blue hijab and reflecting tiny rainbows in the light.

"Mind if I sit here?" I asked, approaching the bench next to the girl.

Surprised, she turned to face me. "Sure." There was a silence between us as I ate my lunch. Her sakura-pink bento box sat empty next to her with small bits of rice left over.

"Farah, right?"

She nodded shyly with a slight grin. "Yes. How do you know my name?"

Breaking eye contact, I looked down at my lunch and admitted, "I saw what happened earlier."

"I see . . ." she said softly.

"Sorry you had to go through that. I've had an encounter with Priya as well in the past. Not the nicest girl."

"Yeah," she agreed. "Her and her girl gang have been the bane of my existence since freshman year. They're on the Academy's senior Equestrian Team and Priya's the captain. In order to participate in extracurricular activities, students must maintain a B average or above."

"Let me guess—she's not very bright."

"Neither her nor her friends' grades are doing well. Rumor has it the coach gave them an ultimatum: either get their grades up by the next report card, or be removed from the team." She glanced down, twiddling her thumbs momentarily before meeting my gaze once again.

"Which is understandable. What does that have to do with you, though?" I queried.

Farah sighed. "Since I help out the head teacher, I have access to the school's grading system. Priya's been pressuring me to go into the system and edit their grades from the last unit's exam. However, it would be way too risky."

"Have you considered notifying your teacher—?"

"It would just make matters worse," she cut in. "She'll make me regret it, I just know it. To keep them off my back, I've been allowing them to copy my notes and homework. Guess that's not enough."

Farah was in a tough position. I felt bad that she feared speaking up. While I couldn't do much about her situation, I figured the least I could do was listen.

"You mustn't allow this to go on, Farah. She'll just keep beating on you if you continue to bend to her will. There will never be an end to it!"

Groaning, she agreed to the obvious. "I know, but how? I don't stand for violence, so I don't want to fight."

"You must fight," I began, "but not physically. You mentioned the coach gave them an ultimatum, correct?"

"Yes."

"And you have access to the grading system, right?"

"Yeah . . ." she trailed off, waiting to see where I was going with this.

"From what you've told me, it appears to me that you have more power than Priya does. Now, the question is, how are you going to use it?"

After putting two and two together, Farah popped up from her seat. "Got it! I know exactly what I'll do. Thanks so much."

"Don't mention it. Sometimes it helps to vent. I'm Elle, by the way."

"Nice to meet you, Elle. Are you new here?"

"I am."

My new friend and I kept each other company for the remainder of lunch. Farah Susanto was the daughter of an Indonesian diplomat. She had enrolled in Rosemary Windsor for the school's STEM program and had been here since freshman year. She was a whiz in math and a member of the school's Science Club. Knowing the school like the back of her hand, she shared important information about the Academy as well as school culture with me as we chatted. Before leaving the rooftop, we both exchanged numbers to keep in touch.

The afternoon session went by fairly quickly, with the remainder of the school day consisting of physical education and calligraphy. Before we were dismissed, all of us broke into various groups for school cleaning. To encourage independence, the Academy encouraged students to lead various activities, and cleaning was one of them. While there were custodians to clean the restrooms, for instance, each class was responsible for keeping their rooms presentable. Student responsibilities were rotated on a monthly basis. As for this month, a couple of other classmates and I were in charge of sanitizing the desks and other surfaces. As the clock struck half past three, the bell rang throughout Rosemary Windsor, signaling the end of the day.

Students flooded into the once deserted halls from the rooms that had held them in captivity for the majority of their day. Full of enthusiasm, they met with their respective cliques and headed off to their cram schools, extracurricular activities, or residences. Due to Jung Hwa's riding practice, Guowei wasn't able to retrieve us until six in the evening.

With our backpacks slung over our shoulders, Farah and Arlo gave me a grand tour of the school, showing me the various clubs around campus. There were many activities available: Photography Club, Music Club, Kendo Club, Rugby Club, Science Club—there was something for everybody. My little tour ended at the bleachers on the soccer field. It was now golden hour, and the sky was a burnt orange. Sitting on the cool metal benches, we watched the girls wearing the white-and-forest-green soccer jerseys run their various drills. Arlo pointed to one girl weaving a ball between yellow cones. "You see that girl over there?" he proudly beamed. "That's my girl, Erin."

Noticing her boyfriend, the peppy brown-eyed redhead waved crazily in our direction. When the Girls' Soccer Club finished practice, she jogged across the field, enthusiastically tackling Arlo in a bear hug.

"Hiya," she greeted. He returned her greeting and embraced her petite frame. Looking over her boyfriend's shoulder, she stared at Farah and me curiously. "Arlo, who are these girls?"

"You know my cousin, yeah? Well, this is one of his clients," he explained, motioning toward me.

After registering what Arlo said, she gasped in shock. "So the rumors are true . . ." she said barely audibly.

"Yep," he confirmed.

Confused, Farah stared at the couple blankly. "What does your cousin do?" she inquired.

"He's a bodyguard for the Royal Family."

"Oh. So, Elle, that means—"

"Yes, my father is Emperor Yamamoto," I admitted.

"Oh, okay . . . well, it's nice to meetcha! Welcome to Rosemary Windsor," Erin said happily.

After we talked with Erin for a bit, Jung Hwa wasted no time in checking up on me. He sent me a quick text after practice concluded and we agreed to meet up at the quad.

Sitting at a table under a humongous cherry blossom tree, we watched the remaining students leaving campus, crowding the walkways of the Sakura-covered cobblestone paths. There was one last organization wrapping up its activities. Members in forest-green armbands and berets were handing out fliers to various passersby.

"Thanks for the tour, guys. The Academy seems to have many clubs."

"No prob," said Farah. "Are there any that interest you?"

"My brother did mention we have a great equestrian program . . ."

"This is a humblebrag, but we are pretty well-known for our sports programming," admitted Erin.

A tall, slender milky-skinned girl with raven locks secured in a long braid approached our table. She sported the same forest-green armband I'd seen people wearing today plus a matching beret. Her eyes scanning me and Farah up and down, she offered only Arlo and Erin a flier, then took her leave. "What was that about?" I questioned as I watched them study the piece of paper.

Arlo's face scrunched in disgust as his eyes scanned the message. Crumpling the document into a ball, he tossed it into the trash bin adjacent to our table. “Nothing,” he muttered. Mimicking her boyfriend’s actions, Erin tossed her flier as well.

“Honestly, I don’t know why that club gets so much support,” Farah murmured, watching as the raven-haired girl met up with her fellow club members. All of them looked almost identical: hair plaited in double braids, berets worn to the side.

“They’re part of the Narean League,” Arlo explained. “They’re student-run, but are backed by the Narean Nationalist Party. They are staunch traditionalists and believe in upholding our nation’s culture and values. Some of their policies are quite controversial. For years, they’ve been pushing a ‘Narea for Nareans’ initiative.”

“Their club upholds their values and offers membership to Narean-born students only,” added Farah. She pointed at me, then herself. “*We* obviously don’t qualify.”

“Not like the League is worth it, anyways,” Arlo declared. We all broke out in laughter, lightening up the mood as my brother approached in his riding gear.

Everyone besides myself stood and greeted my brother formally, bowing slightly. I buried my face in Jung’s chest as he greeted me in a friendly embrace. “How was practice?” I mumbled, looking up at him.

“It was okay. I see you made some friends!”

I introduced him to Farah, Erin, and Arlo. “You’re Guowei’s cousin, yeah?” Jung asked Arlo. “Your family owns that music store.”

“Yeah,” Arlo confirmed. “Elle is in my class, so I thought I’d give her a tour of the campus.”

“I’m glad my sister is in good company! It’s nice meeting you all.”

Exchanging goodbyes with my new companions, we all parted ways for the day. The ride home was long. After sharing the rundown of our days, I rested my head against the tinted car windows and watched the scenery pass by until my eyes fluttered shut.

Later in the evening, my father summoned me to his office.

"Come in," he called after I knocked to announce my arrival. Sitting behind his oak desk, he was accompanied by Ayotola.

"Hey Dad, Ayo."

"Good evening, my daughter. Sit! Tell us about your day."

I planted myself in the vacant plush red velvet chair next to Ayo. "So far, so good."

"I'm glad you're settling in well," said Ayo, relieved.

"As you're aware, the Charity Ball is in a matter of days," my father began.

"Yes, it's this Saturday," I acknowledged.

"A speech has been made for your first public address. Therefore, every afternoon after school, you'll be working with Ayotola so you'll be well prepared for the big day."

And starting the next day, that's exactly what we did. My schedule for the rest of the week was packed to the brim! Ayotola spent two hours with me daily, helping me to rehearse my lines and teach me more social etiquette. I had very little free time, and thus I began to look at my school life as a form of escapism. At Rosemary Windsor, at least, I had the freedom to bask in the company of my newfound friends and engage in the common antics of an adolescent.

Arlo, Erin, Farah and I meet up for lunch on the school roof everyday. Thanks to this trio, I'm adjusting well to student life here. It was a humid and sunny Friday afternoon as Arlo, Erin, and I dug into our meals. Farah rushed over to us, carrying her lunch box. "Elle," She called out to me excitedly. "I did it!" "Did what Farah?" Erin asked in curiosity. "Come on, sit." I offered, "Spill. Tell us everything!" After taking a seat adjacent to me, she proceeded to recount her morning to us.

"Well, this morning, I stopped by Ms. Langsley's before she came in and left a certain someone's failing grades on her desk. After tipping off the head of the Academy's sports programming, I couldn't help but to eavesdrop! About fifteen minutes later, Ms. Langsley came in, and she wasted no time calling Priya to her office. Priya was in utter dismay

That stickler of a PE coach handed the document over to her. 'This was on my desk this morning,' she began. ' I'm sure by now you're well aware of our policy regarding extracurricular activities.'

' How did you get this?' the girl questioned frantically, eyes shifting across the very page that held her test results.

' Who knows? All I know is that this document has the same score that's listed in the database for you, Ms. Singh. As I have stated previously, bad grades equals no sports. You'll be welcome back on the team if your grades improve.'

Priya was such a blubbering mess, pleading with the coach to not remove her from the Equestrian Team. Obviously, it didn't work. Guess the team will be having tryouts soon!" Farah concluded, a devious smirk gracing her face.She was pacifistic in nature and abhorred physical violence, so instead of fighting fire with fire, today she had served justice in her own way. me

"Sweet!" I rejoiced.

"Glad you finally took a stand for yourself, Farah. So now that you got your payback, now what?" Erin questioned while peeling the top off of her steamed cup of ramen.

Farah twiddled her fingers in thought. "Well, just carry on with life, I guess. I just want my last year here to be a peaceful one. Hopefully, this is enough for her to back off."

"I hope so," said Arlo.

"Now, enough about me. How are things going with you, Elle?" Farah asked.

I wrapped some noodles around my fork. "It's going. Ayo's been a taskmaster the last few days."

"Ayo?" Arlo repeated.

"She's my etiquette teacher. I have two-hour lessons every day on top of rehearsals for the Charity Ball this weekend. Father's orders," I vented.

"Sounds exhausting," Farah said.

"It is! On Saturday I have to give an address to the nation. I've been nervous because public speaking has never been a strength of mine. Plus, to make matters worse, members of the Narean Nationalist League will be there."

"Why in the world are those horrible people invited? They hate foreigners," Erin said, shocked.

"This has to be a mistake." Arlo's eyebrows raised in bewilderment. "The Narean Nationalist League has never been invited to past Charity Balls . . . so why now?"

"Who knows? Regardless of whether they show up or not, I plan to keep my distance from them."

"With my cousin watching over you, you'll be fine. I know he wouldn't allow anyone to cause you any harm," Arlo assured me.

"Your cousin's a pretty great guy. He's honestly been grounding me throughout this whole ordeal," I confessed, cheeks becoming a reddish hue.

Seeing my sincerity, Erin got a glint in her eyes and looked over to her boyfriend, nudging him playfully. "Hey, Arlo, I think our friend here is developing feelings for your cousin."

"What?! Erin, no way," I lied, slightly embarrassed.

"You two *have* been spending a lot of time together. Despite being loyal to the crown, Guowei has never spent his free time with a royal," Arlo observed.

"Yep," Erin continued, "what Arlo is trying to say is, *you're different*, Elle. Music, our band—it's a form of escapism for him. He has never let anyone else into that space, let alone a royal. He's really going out of his way for you. This is something Arlo and I are seeing for the first time. You enjoy his company, too, don't you?"

All my friends' eyes focused on me, waiting for my answer. I wished Erin was wrong. Truthfully, I was starting to like Guowei more and more with each passing day. "Of course," I finally admitted. "I mean, we're on the same wavelength—"

"Annnd you've been talking about him. A *lot*," Farah cut in.

She has a point.

"Eleanor likes Guowei Qi!" Erin concluded. "I called it! I'm pretty good at spotting a possible ship, and based on what I see, the *S.S. Elwei* is set to sail!" Farah agreed wholeheartedly.

As I witnessed the excitement shared between the girls, while well-intentioned, I thought to myself, *These two are jumping to conclusions. I may have feelings for Guowei, but there's no telling if he feels the same.* Like an onion, I'd had to slowly peel away so many of his layers before he began to open up to me. Though charming, he was an enigma that I was still trying to figure out.

Playfully rolling my eyes as they laughed, the afternoon bell rang from the top of the bell tower, signaling the conclusion of lunch. *Thank goodness!* Packing our things, we left our meeting spot on the rooftop and headed back downstairs to class.

THE EVENING WAS BUSY. THOUGH I WAS EXHAUSTED FROM MY PRODUCTIVE day at school, I had no time to rest, as Ayo ushered me off to the classroom the moment I got home. Lessons were becoming more extensive with each passing day, and besides rehearsing my speech for the weekend, tonight's itinerary also included ballroom dancing lessons.

"We thought it would be nice to have a father-daughter dance. It'd be a sweet family moment to air to the masses," Ayo said excitedly. "Are you familiar with the waltz?"

"I've heard of it, but never done it," I said simply. "Where do I begin?"

"Simple. First, you need a partner." Heading to the door, Ayo invited in Guowei, who stood right outside.

"I'm assuming that would be me," said Guowei.

A playful smirk tugged on Ayo's lips as she glanced between my bodyguard and me. "Indeed."

After explaining and briefly demonstrating the dance steps, she directed us to attempt to recreate the choreography. A soft, calming instrumental melody hummed throughout the room as stars shone brightly in the navy-blanketed sky outside the palace. Placing my hand into his, he whisked me away, smoothly moving us across the floor. Sweetly gazing into his eyes, I fully surrendered myself, allowing him to take the lead. "Not so bad, huh?" he asked.

"Guess not. Sort of like playing a game of follow-the-leader," I replied.

"Hmm, that's a nice way to put it. I guess I'm it."

Our playful banter continued on, both of us somewhat forgetting the presence beside ourselves in the room. As the melodic tune concluded, Ayo's steady claps reverberated off the walls. "Well done, you two!"

With one hand still clasped with mine and the other on the small of my back, Guowei inched forward until our foreheads touched. "Thank you," I smiled.

"The pleasure was all mine."

CHAPTER EIGHT

MEJO

Empress Angeline

Saturday was hectic. While Elle was preoccupied with preparing for the evening, her stepmother, Empress Angeline, sat in her sitting room on her plush loveseat. Accompanied by her son and her husband's second-in-command, they proceeded to discuss their grand plan.

It was perfectly crafted. Due to the sudden appearance of her stepdaughter in her abode, her son's place in line to the throne had been pushed back. Due to written Narean law, if the current emperor were to pass on, the firstborn was first in line to the throne, regardless of gender. Despite the Young Miss coming into the world prior to her parent's marital vows, Eleanor still posed a threat in taking the very spot the empress had worked so diligently to procure for her son.

"Mum, do we really have to do this?" her son questioned. Jung Hwa was between a rock and a hard place. He cared for his sister, but he had also been raised to be loyal to his mother. For years now, he had kept his head low, enjoying his mostly private life away from the spotlight. To appease his mother and gain respect from his biological father, he constantly walked a tightrope to meet their expectations. A feeling of immense guilt weighed upon his shoulders as he paced steadily in contemplation.

Angeline's cold, soulless gaze bored into her son's earth-tone eyes. "After all these years I've worked to get you here, absolutely. Remember, this won't just secure your future—it will also preserve the purity of the Royal Family's bloodline. Elle is a stain on the once pristine fabric of this family, and like all stains, she'll be removed. With or without your father's support." Turning her attention to her husband's closest confidante, she asked curtly, "I'm assuming all is in order, Mr. Yao?"

A man of very few words, Mr. Yao hummed in confirmation, lifting the falling metal frame of his glasses up his nose. The reflection of the crystal chandelier that hung from the high-rise ceiling reflected off them. "T-There's nothing to be worried about, Your Highness," the man stuttered. "I can assure you things will go well tonight."

Rising, she sauntered over to the man, who refused to meet her gaze. "As they must. I'm glad we have such a great and intimate bond, Mr. Yao. I mean, any little sign of hesitation would force me to release all the evidence I have on you to your wife." Resting her hands on his chest, she looked up to meet his rain-colored eyes.

"What are you talking about? You came on to me!" he hissed in disbelief.

"According to you. It's my word against yours, so you might want to play your cards right."

ELEANOR & GUOWEI

Just down the hall, Elle was in her room with the Ross sisters. As usual, the two younger sisters verbally sparred back and forth while the eldest finished laying out the gown and numerous accessories left for Elle by Ayotola. The stylist had settled on a strapless bell-shaped gown in lavender, accompanied by a matching shawl. The shimmering tulle overlaid a silk lining that reached down to the floor. Miniature boxes of black velvet held the diamond statement pieces that would soon grace the Young Miss. To ease her nerves, the most recent Onew solo vinyl—gifted to her by Arlo—played faintly in the background, the music floating through the room. She hummed along to each song, occasionally softly singing along to a chorus or two.

With her hair in a curly pineapple on top of her head, she indulged in her beauty treatments adorned in an eggshell nightgown. A glam team, along with hairstylists, were due to arrive early in the evening to prepare the young royal for the event ahead.

"Goodness, this dress is absolutely gorgeous," gushed Elle, admiring the gown draped across her bed. Sunlight shined in through the open terrace doors. The ladies were greeted with the occasional summer breeze that found its way into the bedroom.

After a gentle knock at the door, Guowei entered. Racing over to him, Elle wrapped the gentle giant in a bear hug. Returning her embrace, he affectionately patted the fluffy cloud of S-shaped curls on top of her head. "Good morning," he greeted Elle.

"Morning," she said sweetly.

"So, today's the day. Are you ready?"

"As I'll ever be. I'm still nervous, Guowei."

"That's only natural, but I and many others have confidence you'll do well tonight."

"That's right," Everleigh chimed, "you'll be phenomenal! I just know it!"

"Thanks, guys."

"So, what's today's agenda?" asked Guowei.

"Nothing much besides the ball tonight. The girls just set out my outfit, and now we're just chilling until the hair and makeup team comes this afternoon."

"Sounds good. Once you finish up, meet me downstairs in the courtyard."

"Why the courtyard?" Elle inquired while slowly rolling up and down on the balls of her feet.

"There's a surprise for you out there."

"Okay . . . well, I guess I'll see you then." The Young Miss backed away playfully while the well-decorated guard took his leave, not forgetting to close the door behind him.

His white-gloved hand reached into his breast pocket, pulling out a small box. A smile graced his lips as he peeked inside. Sweet memories of the night prior crossed his mind, yet another perfect night among the other lovely moments shared between them. Satisfied with its contents, he placed it back into his coat pocket and marched along, going about his day.

EMPEROR YAMAMOTO

As one of the most televised events in the country, there was around-the-clock news coverage of the ball from both domestic and international media stations. Security had been tightened, with guards placed strategically throughout the palace. Besides the reports and onlookers, there were also protesters stationed right outside the gates of the palace. The Royal Guards separated them from the entrance, but passionate chants and insults betrayed their presence. Luckily, their remarks were barely audible from where Eleanor was.

With all his daughter had had to endure over the past few months, her father tried his best to shield his child from the vitriolic attacks from both fringe media and some of Narea's own citizens.

Presently, Emperor Yamamoto was going over the final touches for the grand occasion, meeting with both General Singh and Mr. Yao, respectively. He peeked outside his office window at the various news anchors and camera crews stationed outside the gates, along with the common citizens who had started gathering the evening prior.

While this was largely a celebratory occasion, the emperor was not ignorant of the opposition from some. The loudest voice on the opposing side was naturally the Narean Nationalist League, a prominent party that constantly spoke out on the country's immigration policy. In their eyes, having a princess not of pure Narean blood would not only bring shame and dishonor to the Royal Family, but to their entire nation.

Unfortunately, Hironori was very familiar with their sentiment, as these were the same beliefs his parents had held. When they had discovered the existence of Elle, they had done their utmost to scrub any inkling of her from the public eye. They'd wanted no association at all with their granddaughter, but despite all of this, Hironori had secretly maintained contact with his former fiancée's family and watched Eleanor grow up from the shadows.

He had funded her extracurricular and academic endeavors, providing her with nothing short of the best. Only having a box full of photographs over the years to make him feel connected to his little girl, he cared immensely for his daughter, and he was determined to create a more welcoming and tolerant nation by the time she reached adulthood.

Despite his parents' passing, their legacy of national superiority remained. "Narea for Nareans"—that was what his parents had stood for, and now the very party his mother had founded continued to uphold their ideology.

After the death of Abioye, a passionate fire burned in his heart. After his parents passed, he diligently changed the many controversial policies that were once in place. Now, many years later, the country has welcomed people of all kinds and is considered one of the most diverse nations in the world. Hironori Yamamoto, by all accounts, was a successful man.

"General Singh, how are the security preparations for this evening?"

"Security has been doubled around the property, sir, and tripled at the event location," Mr. Singh reported.

The emperor nodded. "Mr. Yao, my friend of many years. How much time do we have?"

"We must now get ready, sir. We are scheduled to leave at six to begin the procession."

Hironori glanced down at his watch. "Ah, yes, you're right. But first, gentlemen, we drink!" Grabbing a bottle of his favorite cognac, he poured everyone a drink, serving himself last. "Tonight will be a joyous occasion, and finally my firstborn child will be by my side." He smiled to himself, thinking that if she were still alive, Abioye would be so proud. *If only she had lived to see her daughter's accomplishments.*

ELLE

At dusk, Elle thanked the Ross sisters for their work and went to meet Guowei in the courtyard, as promised. Her gold heels clicked on the white marble floors, announcing her presence as she weaved through the halls. Palace maids and other staff greeted the girl as she gracefully stepped out onto the concrete deck and carefully descended the stairs onto the gray cobblestone path.

There was a faint neigh in the distance. Not yet seeing her friend and bodyguard, she decided to continue onward to the gardens.

Picking up the front of her dress, she was careful not to get any grass stains or marks on the glimmering lavender gown. Her curly locks cascaded down to her lower back, a lavender and gold crown pinned to her head. Going around the hedges and meticulously cut shrubbery, there stood Guowei and a stable hand who held the reins to a beautiful brown-coated Arabian.

Elle admired the horse's beauty, raven-black hair and all. "It's beautiful," she gasped.

Guowei watched the beautiful girl in awe as she petted the horse's mane. "Looks like you like him," he said.

"I love him!" she exclaimed happily, trying to hold back joyous tears. "I've always wanted my own horse. This is a wonderful surprise—thank you so much."

"Well, I'm glad you like it. However, this gift is from your father. Now this," he said, pulling the small box out of his suit pocket, "is from me." He handed over the box secured with a lilac satin ribbon, placing it into the young and humble royal's open palms.

Elle gracefully received her gift with both hands, as she had been trained by Ayo per royal etiquette. Gently pulling the ribbon, she lifted the lid to reveal a simple gold bracelet that had a message inscribed in Guowei's native language. She delicately picked it up and studied the piece of metal. "It's gorgeous! Thank you." Her heels making her the same height as Guowei, she linked her arms around his neck, hugging him. "I'm afraid I can't read the message inscribed. What does it say?"

Before the young man could provide a translation, Soo-Young and Emperor Yamamoto entered the garden. "Young Miss, don't you look beautiful!" Soo-Young called.

Quickly, the two took a couple of steps back from each other, both parties' cheeks turning red. Guowei looked down, finding his shoes more interesting. "Thanks, Soo-Young," said the young girl softly.

Soo-Young suspiciously looked between the two young people, deciding to not question what she had just witnessed—at least, not in Elle's presence. Today was special, after all, and Guowei's and Elle's developing romantic interest in one another was the least of her concerns at the moment. The subject would have to be brought up eventually, but for now, she was focused on preparing Elle mentally for some of the vitriol she may be forced to hear leaving the property.

"Well *someone* looks fancy," Elle greeted her father, who donned a black tuxedo.

"Thanks, dear," he said warmly, pecking his daughter on the cheek. "The procession will start soon. We better get going."

Leaving the chocolate Arabian horse in the care of the stable hand, everyone headed back to the palace, meeting both Jung Hwa and Angeline in the foyer. Walking slightly behind her father, stepmother, and Soo-Young, nerves began to build up in the young girl, who was weary of the unknown. She walked beside her elder brother, not knowing he was dealing with his own mental battle and immense guilt.

Jung Hwa's brown irises glanced over to his nervous sister. Sensing her anxiety, he silently reached over and held her little clenched hand. "It'll be okay," he softly assured her, interrupting her inner doubts and all the what-ifs.

Led by Clydesdales, lily-white chrysanthemum-adorned carriages were parked outside, waiting for their passengers. The emperor halted and turned swiftly before adventuring outside. Facing his family, he proceeded to address his daughter directly. "My child, the time has come for you to join this family on your first engagement. Words cannot describe how proud I am of you. Remember, regardless of what you may hear beyond that door, know you are well loved."

"Members of the Narean Party are protesting outside. Whatever they say, do not engage with them, and stay close to the guards," Soo-Young instructed. After the signal from Guowei, the guards opened the door, exposing the family to the world beyond.

In case of a tragic event in which a family member perishes, it was protocol for the royals to travel separately in pairs. Taking the lead, Emperor Yamamoto and Empress Angeline took their first steps outside the palace. Greeting the drivers, they stepped into the first carriage along with Soo-Young. After they got settled, Jung Hwa stepped out, with Elle following close behind with Guowei. The trio settled into the carriage behind the emperor and empress.

Trying her best to not let her nerves get the best of her, Elle took slow, steady breaths, looking blankly forward. "Elle, look at me," Guowei whispered. Her earthen eyes glanced over at the stoic man who exuded outward strength. He gently grasped her hand on the seat. "It's okay. When going up there tonight, look straight ahead, not down. Never let your crown fall."

"Guowei's right," her brother chimed in. "Never allow anyone to make your crown fall. Not even those you love."

"Alright . . . let's go, gentlemen," the girl softly whispered, head held high.

After Eleanor Yamamoto exited the gates, there was no going back. Now she was at the point of no return, and the only direction to go was forward.

Trumpets triumphantly sounded throughout the area as the carriages began to move toward the gates. Cheers and chants became louder the closer the passengers got. The horses marched on at a steady pace, pulling the carriages forward. For her protection, Elle was sandwiched between Guowei and Jung Hwa. Elle continued looking forward, holding the hands of both her bodyguard and her brother for reassurance. Guowei's thumb traced small circles on her hand to keep her calm.

"Citizens of Narea," a male guard announced, "make way for the Royal Family!" The armed guardsmen formed a straight line between the closed iron gates and the protesters stomping loudly before marching forward. The crowd began to move back the closer the intimidating guards got.

"Back away, behind the designated line!" another commanded.

Once it was ensured that all spectators were in their designated places, a guard taking the lead turned from the line, stomping to the middle of the road. After barking a few more commands, the two guardsmen opened the gate. "Continue onward!" With another triumphant melody from the trumpeters, the carriages one by one moved forward. Drummer boys led the procession followed by the trumpeters, then the flower girls. Finally, as their carriages rolled by, there was an overwhelming swell of cheers and support. Citizens offered countless gifts for the family that were promptly collected by the security guards on foot.

The grand spectacle continued on until coming to a halt at the Unification Museum. The gray stone building was illuminated by white lights. Footmen rolled out the red carpet that led to the entrance, and the little flower girls, who appeared no older than six years, lined up to the side, two girls per carriage. As the emperor and empress disembarked from the carriage, the two small girls curtsied in front of them and then walked slowly ahead side by side, tossing yellow chrysanthemum petals as Narea's royals followed behind.

"The little ones are adorable," gushed Elle, watching the children dressed in matching white sundresses and holding wicker baskets.

Guowei nodded. "They're from one of the orphanages we're raising money for. Dad and Mum handpick the kids each year."

"Ah, how nice."

News commentators nearby gave a play-by-play of the event, announcing the guests of honor as they arrived. Before exiting the vehicle, Jung Hwa turned to his sister, knowing it would be their last positive exchange between each other. "Hey, Elle," he said softly.

"Yes, Jung?"

"You look beautiful. You're going to be great tonight."

"Thank you for all your support. You've helped me so much since coming here! I'm proud to call you my older brother. I love you."

A stab of guilt hit the man, hearing his sister's sweet confession. "Don't mention it, sis. I love you too." With nothing left to say, Jung Hwa stepped down from the carriage, greeting some onlookers and guests.

"Her Highness Princess Eleanor Aurora Yamamoto of Narea!" Once Elle's gold diamond-studded heels stepped onto the red carpet, the media finally got the opportunity to see the rumored hidden child of the emperor up close. Like a deer caught in headlights, the girl stayed in her spot, a smile plastered on her face, as cameramen began hounding her with their flashing lights.

After a few shots were taken of the princess, Guowei guided her through the crowd to the entrance. The whole family was gathered together, grinning widely for the press. A small girl with a caramel complexion and her hair braided into a halo greeted the Young Miss with a curtsy, offering Eleanor a bouquet of bright yellow chrysanthemums, the country's national flower. Onlookers gushed over the girl's sweet gesture as Elle accepted the gift with grace, kindly thanking her.

Basking in the constant attention and adoration, little did Elle know she was to soon be betrayed. With an arm around his daughter, the emperor led her into the ball, beckoning the royalty of other nations and domestic elites in attendance to meet his firstborn child. Most welcomed the new girl into their close-knit social circle, striking up friendly conversations over a drink of champagne.

The venue was decorated with chrysanthemums throughout. The Yamamoto family seal was projected onto the tile floor and large candelabras served as the centerpieces of the lavender tables scattered throughout, surrounding the dance floor. The stage sat at the very front, where a string quartet played sweet melodies while guests continued to intermingle.

Tonight's menu was a fusion of both traditional and modern, the chefs serving cultural dishes with a modernized twist. One of Narea's most influential personalities Sir Amadeus took center stage, introducing a variety of acts organized by various children's homes in the area. First, Unification City's Youth Choir lifted their voices, opening the show with a well-known folk song and then transitioning to a tune specifically composed for the evening. There were tiny dancers, pianists, and collaborative performances amongst the vast menagerie of talent displayed for the nation to see.

The Yamamotos were quite entertained, watching in awe along with the other attendees. Just before dinner was served, Hironori stood from his seat, the crowd cheering as they watched their emperor approach the mic center stage accompanied by Angeline and Mr. Yao, each holding a flute of bubbling champagne.

"Good evening, and thank you for coming to tonight's ball! For the past twenty years, my family has partnered with the local orphanages in the area to raise money, as well as allow an opportunity for some of Narea's incredible children to be showcased. Every bright young performer you've seen tonight is currently up for adoption," Elle's father informed the crowd. "This year's twentieth celebration is bigger than ever. Parenthood is indeed a gift—a blessing! I know this for a fact, as I'm a father myself. This nation has followed and supported my stepson, Jung Hwa, ever since his mother and I became a family unit. Tonight, it's my pleasure to present to you, for the first time, my daughter—Eleanor Aurora Yamamoto, Princess of Narea!"

On cue, Elle was escorted to the stage by Jung Hwa, who offered his arm to his younger sister for support. The world watched her closely, attentively, as she took her position amongst her family onstage.

With a spotlight shining from above and a teleprompter not far from her, Elle was ready to deliver her first address. Arlo, Erin, and Farah as well as Elle's family and friends back in America tuned into the broadcast from their homes as the cameras zoomed in on the teen girl in the midst of the rich and powerful. After a deep breath, she began to deliver a speech of peace, tolerance, and hope for a better future.

Her father had been successful in meeting his goal of making Narea a nation of increased tolerance; however, with the ongoing protests from the opposing fringe minority, there were clearly still some old ways of thinking present. Underneath all the music, the glamour, and the mass adoration, the young teenage girl was aware of the intense hatred some had for her solely due to her caramel complexion. It pained her heart that people could hold such hatred for their fellow humans. Such thinking was absurd, in her opinion. Just like her father, she, too, had the same dream of seeing Narea become a nation of true unity. Like Narea's yellow chrysanthemums, Elle wished her nation to know happiness and its citizens to enjoy friendship amongst all peoples, regardless of their skin color or nationality.

Not so far away, Guowei's attention was divided as he watched Elle deliver her speech. He communicated back and forth with other guardsmen, making sure everything was secure. Security had been tripled for the safety of the Royal Family. Under General Singh's command, no one could come in or out once the event had commenced. Elle's smooth, high-pitched voice echoed off the walls of the museum, silencing the faint chants coming from outside. At the conclusion of her speech, the inspired audience erupted into applause. A feeling of relief washed over the girl; now, she was at peace.

ANGELINE POURED HER HUSBAND A FRESH GLASS OF CHAMPAGNE, encouraging her husband to drink and celebrate this special occasion. As the audience continued their praise, Hironori took a few sips of his drink, admiring his daughter's accomplishment. This was only the very beginning. He had so much more he wanted to accomplish, and he was happy to have the privilege of doing so with his daughter by his side.

The sounds from the crowd began to blur in his mind, their voices sounding like echoes. Chills shot through his body, and his heartbeat began to quicken. Angeline spoke to her husband, but what she said to him was unknown. Confused and frightened, Hironori attempted to form words but he started to slur, no longer comprehensible. Knowing very well what was happening to his dad, Jung Hwa looked down at his shoes, not wanting to see what was to happen next.

Hearing a loud thump and the crash of glass shattering on stage, Elle turned away from the rolling cameras. "Dad!" she gasped as she rushed to her father's side. Lying on the floor, Hironori attempted to plead for help. Frightened by the turn of events, Elle unleashed a scream for the guards, immediately alerting Guowei and the others.

Despite all the safety measures taken, Narea's own emperor's life was now in danger. *Who could possibly be responsible for this?* Tears blurred Elle's eyes as she continued speaking to her father, pleading for him to stay with her. She called for help on his behalf as the horrified witnesses made room for the various medics and security on staff.

Soo-Young rushed to Elle's side. "Cut the cameras!" she ordered.

Angeline stooped down by her husband, holding his hand and feeling his weak pulse. No tears were shed; on the contrary, his wife internally rejoiced as her plan came to fruition. "My love, hang in there. Help is on the way," she said calmly, leaning down to peck Hiro's cheek.

With Elle looking to both her stepbrother and stepmother for comfort, Jung Hwa went to her, consoling Elle as the medics placed their father on a stretcher before taking him away. "Jung Hwa, I thought everything was safe. Who did this to Dad?" Elle asked, bewildered. *Who could've possibly done this?!* she thought to herself as she watched her father's consciousness fade.

"I'm not sure," the girl's stepbrother fibbed. Arms wrapped around her, Jung Hwa embraced the emotional girl, guilt eating away at him with each growing second.

Angeline went to her husband on the stretcher, once more taking his hand. "Your Highness," said one of the medical personnel, "Emperor Yamamoto's oxygen level is low. We must go to the hospital immediately!"

"Please do what you can," Empress Angeline pleaded. Stepping away from her husband, she went to meet her son near Elle, Soo-Young, and Guowei.

"Angeline, how's Dad?" Elle asked, tears staining her face.

"Not so well. They're taking him to the hospital. We should start heading over there."

"I'll get security to escort you," offered Guowei. Within moments, the royals were all ushered into separate vehicles with dark-tinted windows parked in the back of the museum. Elle's stepbrother and stepmother rode together, leaving Soo-Young and Eleanor in Guowei's care. Emergency sirens lit the way in blue and red as the two sedans closely followed one another.

Soo-Young tried comforting the young lady as they sat in the back seat. The girl had cried so much, that she had run out of tears. She looked listless, occasionally sniffling as she rested her head on the cold glass window. Once at the hospital, they were led into a private waiting area. Until Hironori was stabilized, no one except hospital staff was allowed in his room.

Time seemed to pass by slowly until one of the doctors dressed in white entered the waiting room, catching everyone's attention. "Doctor, how's my father doing?" Eleanor asked, concern etched on her soft features.

"Well, I have some good news. My team and I have successfully stabilized the emperor, and his oxygen levels have improved."

"That's wonderful!" she said, relieved.

"When can we see him?" Angeline asked, a soulless smile tugging at her lips.

"Now, if you'd like."

"That'd be lovely, thank you." Everyone, royals and guards alike, quickly stood up, eager to see the emperor.

"Two visitors at a time, please," the doctor requested.

Without skipping a beat, Eleanor, Jung Hwa, and Angeline stepped forward. The Young Miss's eyebrows knitted together as she looked over to her stepbrother, pleading silently to visit with her father. The young man cursed under his breath, knowing very well that the time had finally come for him to part ways with his little stepsister. Before he could say anything, his mother stepped in. "Elle," the woman began, placing her hand on her stepdaughter's shoulder, "Jung Hwa and I will go first. You can see your father afterward."

Despite being disappointed, the young girl didn't object. While they didn't have the best relationship, Angeline was her father's wife, after all. *They're probably just as concerned as I am.* "Okay, I'll stay," she conceded.

Taking one last glance at Eleanor, Jung Hwa followed both his mother and the doctor through the double doors, allowing them to close automatically behind him.

"How is he *really*?" Angeline asked the doctor.

"See for yourself, Your Highness. You administered the poison well."

Stopping in front of a window, they peered into a room. Within it lay a weak and defenseless Hironori Yamamoto. His lids concealed his eyes as his chest steadily moved up and down with each inhale and exhale, his body connected to a machine to be closely monitored. A serpent-like smile appeared on the empress's lips. Now, with Hironori out of the picture, her son could finally rule with the possession of his stepfather's signet ring. A sacred heirloom that had been passed down from ruler to ruler, whoever wore this ring wielded immense power.

"Just look at him," she began. "He's a vegetable at this point! Looks like our great kingdom needs another leader. Someone like Jung Hwa is just what our country needs!" She glanced over at her son quietly standing by, looking at his stepfather.

The very man who had been more involved in his life than his biological dad was comatose thanks to him. Instead of thinking of his betrayal, he is mentally disassociated to follow in his mother's footsteps. *Sometimes, one must sacrifice others to succeed,* the young man mentally told himself.

"Did you get the ring?" the empress asked. Reaching into his pocket, the doctor pulled out the intricate band of gold, planting it in Angeline's palm. "My gift from me to you, my son. Now that we've got what we need, maybe it's time we see that stepsister of yours." After thanking the doctor, both mother and son headed back to the waiting area.

The laws of the land were very specific, but Angeline knew how far to go to get what she wanted. If Emperor Yamamoto were to die, then by law, Eleanor would qualify to take the throne by birthright as his only biological child. She needed for the emperor to be not only out of the picture, but also kept alive, creating the perfect "unfortunate" circumstances for Jung Hwa's takeover.

In the waiting room, Elle rested her head on Guowei's shoulder. After worrying so much over her father, the young lady was exhausted. "Guowei," she mumbled. He hummed in response. "How long has it been? Since they went back there?"

He glanced up at the clock on the pristine white wall. "It's been a couple of hours. I'm glad the medical staff was able to stabilize the emperor."

"Me too . . . but I'm still wondering how all this happened. I was there when my father and General Singh were planning the security measures," said Elle.

"With this many security personnel on staff this evening, it would've been impossible for someone from the outside to infiltrate the ball. Nothing would've gotten past us—"

"That's the thing, Guowei. Like you said, it would've been *impossible* for someone from the outside. Which means there's a rat among us," Soo-Young concluded. "The question is . . . who?"

As if on command, Angeline strutted through the double doors with her son not far behind. Soo-Young, Guowei, and Elle stood up to greet them. "Your Highness," the bodyguard greeted.

"How's Dad?" Elle asked her stepmother.

"Your father's fine," she replied plainly.

"I'm relieved. Well, Guowei and I are going to visit with him a bit. If you will excuse us—"

"Hmm, I think not," the empress countered.

"But you said I could see him after you and Jung Hwa."

"Well, I lied."

The princess was confused by the passive-aggressive nature of her stepmother. Yes, neither lady was fond of the other, but Eleanor believed they shared at least one thing in common: they both loved her father. As reasonable as she was, Eleanor's frustration turned to rage. Even Soo-Young could not hold her back. "What happened just a few hours ago *mortified* me! I've already lost my mother—I'm just glad Dad is safe! I'm well aware you dislike me, Angeline, but I implore you, *please* let me see my father!"

A loud slap was heard throughout the space as Angeline's manicured hands made contact with Elle's face. Speechless, the girl put a hand up to her stinging cheek. Feeling hot tears brewing in her eyes, she refused to let them fall.

"Your Highness, that was uncalled for," Guowei said in the girl's defense. Taking Elle's hand, he led her closer to the double doors. "Let's go, Elle, we're seeing your father."

"Absolutely not! You two aren't going anywhere" she began. "GUARDS, block the exit!"

On command, guardsmen blocked the only way out of the waiting room. Guowei and Elle glanced at each other. Neither said anything, but both instantly put two and two together. "Oh my goodness, *you* did this," the girl said in disbelief. "But why?"

"Why? Hiro is a millstone around my neck," Angeline seethed. "He always talked about his hopes and aspirations for you. It disgusted me that he would go as far as changing royal policy to make you next in line to rule, skipping over my son, who would be a far superior emperor. I played along with you and your father for a bit, but now playtime's over. Like I stated the first day we met: You are not welcome here. You're not worthy to take the throne, and I'll do everything in my power to make sure that never happens!" Ring in hand, she moved to place it on her son's hand. "Call security to take them away!"

"Mum . . ." Jung Hwa pleaded.

"It's either us or them. Do as I say, boy," she instructed.

"Jung Hwa!" his sister called, trying to get her brother's attention.

Tuning out her voice and refusing to acknowledge her, he obeyed his mother's demand. "Take them away," he commanded the guards.

Showing hesitancy, the guardsmen were confused by the prince's odd request. "My prince," a random guard defended, "she's your sister—"

"*Step*sister," Jung Hwa emphasized. "Last time I checked, I was an only child. I hold the signet ring of my father; now, my word is absolute. Take them away!" On his second command, the guards surrounded Elle, Soo-Young, and Guowei, forcefully taking them back to the palace.

Chapter Nine

Mesan

The very place that was once a luxurious paradise became a prison overnight as the three of us were locked in an all-white windowless room beneath the palace. I had never seen this area before, but being confined to the blank white space was slowly chipping away at my sanity.

"Forty-eight hours," I said plainly.

"What?" Soo-Young asked me from the other side of the cell.

"They've kept us here for forty-eight hours. I've counted. We need to find a way out of here. Who knows what my brother and stepmom are up to?"

Still in our formal wear from the ruined ball, Guowei, Soo-Young, and I sat on the white concrete-covered floor. "Impossible,"

Guowei stated, "They've put us in the box. This is where we put criminals. There's only one way out."

"Maybe you can think of something?" Soo-Young suggested, trying to hold on to one thread of hope. "Guowei, you used to be posted here quite a bit. You know this place like the back of your hand. Come on, think!"

"Hmm . . . there is one way. Who'd like to play sick for a bit?"

Both of us looked blankly at Guowei. "Sick?"

"If an inmate is ill, we temporarily release them from their cell for medical treatment. I think I can get us out safely by creating a diversion," Guowei proposed. "If one of us acts like they're sick, we can convince the guard on duty to open the door. Then, from there, we can fight our way to the exit. So, ladies, what do you say?"

I looked over to Soo-Young. "We're in," we both said in unison.

"Good. So, who's ill?" Without hesitation, I raised my hand, silently volunteering myself for the role.

In hushed tones, all three of us went over our game plan. "The only exit is the same way we got in here. Elle, once you start choking, Soo-Young will get the guard's attention. When he opens our cell, let's all grab him, then lock him in. Once he's secured, all there's left to worry about are the two checkpoints. Typically, there are two guards at each. If we can work together to fight them off, then—"

"We'll be home free," I finished.

The man nodded. "Precisely, Princess. The exit leads to the throne room. Once we get out of here, then we'll figure out what to do next."

"Sounds easier said than done. You're forgetting guards that are posted here are armed," hissed Soo-Young.

I glanced back at the door with growing apprehension. Perhaps the ambassador was right. How could three people take on a group of armed guardsmen? Biting my bottom lip, I began to panic. But before my mind could further strike fear in me, creating possible atrocious scenarios as to what could happen, Guowei placed both of his hands on my shoulders.

"Elle, I know what you're thinking. I know you're afraid, but you must trust me fully for this to work."

Both of our foreheads touched as we gazed into each other's eyes. Tears slid down my cheeks. "I'm terrified."

"I know," he reaffirmed.

"What if one of us gets killed?"

"It won't happen. I won't allow it." After wiping away my tears, he pecked my forehead. "Remember, don't let your crown fall, Princess. Everything will be okay. I promise."

Sniffling softly, I nodded my head. "Okay . . . I'll trust you."

Backing away slowly, I began to pretend I was choking, *loudly*. Getting into position, Guowei backed up to the side of the door as Soo-Young proceeded to plead for help. Hearing all the choking and hacking in the blank white cell, the guard on duty opened the eye slot to peek through at the trio. "Quiet down!" the gruff voice bellowed from the other side.

"Can't you see she's choking? She can't breathe! Help her!" Soo-Young said frantically, meeting the guard's gaze.

Opening the door and rushing in, the man called out to the other guards, "Quick! Get the palace doctor!"

JUNG HWA

Higher up in the palace, Jung-Hwa sat alone in his room while Eden the handmaiden prepared the empress for the evening in her quarters. Unlike his sister's physical captivity, Jung Hwa's was more of a figurative one—the prison of the mind. Alone he sat on the couch, head held in his hands as he watched the ongoing news coverage that was playing on most citizens' television sets.

The growing pain of guilt weighed heavily on his heart as his mind replayed the plot that had unfolded two nights prior. The sudden turn of events had left the majority of citizens shell-shocked. Footage of the em-

peror falling ill had been captured for all to see during the Charity Ball, but while the citizens of Narea were being kept in the dark, the palace staff was fully aware of what the mother and son duo had done.

Despite the clear and incriminating evidence, no charges were pressed; the power of the signet ring was absolute. The atmosphere had quickly shifted within the palace walls, leaving the staff on edge due to the sudden loss of their emperor. While no one dared to retaliate out of fear of what Angeline was capable of, soft whispers and murmurs of disdain were exchanged amongst the Chrysanthemum Palace's residents. The evil empress's prior actions proved just how low she could stoop to get what she wanted. However, many were puzzled as to how the prince could do such a thing. A kind-natured, generous, and well-mannered boy, he was often praised by others for his achievements and good behavior growing up. Jung Hwa, as such, was very obedient and respected his mother despite their differing views on some things. He was upheld as the nation's golden child, yet behind this idealized persona was an imperfect young man with his own share of flaws.

In this world, there are both leaders and followers. One must have integrity, humility, courage, and strong morals to properly lead the charge. One must show no fear to speak up on what's wrong or right, even in unfavorable times. Unfortunately, the prince did not possess this quality. He was well aware of right and wrong, yet remained a complicit party in the incapacitation of his stepfather and the ousting of his sister, the rightful heir to the throne. It was a mental battle to be obedient in such circumstances. Never before had he disobeyed his mother . . . but perhaps this would be the very straw that broke the camel's back.

A brilliant ray of sunshine, Eleanor brought light to the lives of nearly anyone she crossed paths with. Her sweet and pleasant way of being brightened up the residents' day and made royal life a tad more interesting. Since her arrival, she had grown on him, and deep down he missed her dearly. He knew when they had parted ways for the last time that he would have to break her heart. The girl deserved none of this treatment.

No longer satisfied to be his mum's caged bird, Jung Hwa proceeded to do the unthinkable. Shutting off the television, he stormed out of his room, determined to put a stop to the second part of the empress's plan.

Jung Hwa was met with a commotion in the halls. Many armed guards rushed in the direction of the holding cells, pushing aside any maids or staff that were in the way. Seeing a crying Eden on the sidelines, he approached her. "Hey, what's going on?" he asked the hysterical child.

Shaken, Eden hesitated to respond. She remained on the floor hugging her injured knee, whimpering softly. "You really liked my sister . . . you wanna know a secret? So do I." Getting down to her level, he wiped away the streaming tears in an attempt to comfort her. "I'm going to fix this. However, I need to know what's going on before I can move forward. Do you happen to know why we have a sudden influx of guards?"

Shaking with slight hiccups, Eden looked at the armed men rushing down the hall. Finally meeting Jung Hwa's eyes, she barely spoke, "They're trying to escape. Earlier while I was doing Empress Angeline's hair, I overheard the news from Mr. Yao and General Singh. I fear they might kill them."

After picking the petite girl up and dusting her off, he thanked her and headed straight for the cells. He could hear his sister, Soo-Young, and Guowei the closer he got. By the time Jung Hwa made it past the barrier, the prince was mortified by the scene laid out before him.

The three had managed to escape their imprisonment, Guowei holding a guardsmen's gun they had evidently stolen, and were only a few feet away from the exit that would lead to their freedom. Relief washed over Jung Hwa's face as he saw that his sister wasn't injured; Guowei and Soo-Young, however, were less fortunate. All of their dress clothes were in a disarray, with Guowei's white shirt stained slightly with either his or someone else's blood.

The two stood resolutely in front of Elle, determined to protect the soon-to-be princess from any harm. The armed guards blocking the exit raised their weapons at the trio, threatening to shoot. Putting the stolen gun to use, Guowei returned the favor by firing a warning shot without hesitation, maiming a sole guard's leg. Blood stained the man's pants as he collapsed, yelping in agony as the blood dripped from his wound and pooled on the gray concrete floor.

With that, a battle ensued, as some of the guards lunged towards the trio, attempting to subdue their threat before another one of their comrades got hurt. In hot pursuit, Soo-Young wrestled her opponent's gun away. the trio catapulted into action in a whirlwind of limbs and sheer audacity, hell-bent on disarming their adversaries. A chaotic brawl erupted as the guards fired wildly in a desperate bid to control the unruly prisoners.

The metallic symphony of bullet shells echoed off the corridor walls, some finding their mark in Soo-Young's lily-white skin. Her face contorted in pain, yet an unyielding desperation for freedom fueled her relentless fight against the impending darkness.

Regardless of the consequences, all three fiercely fought on, yet they were clearly outnumbered. Jung Hwa could see their desperation, especially Guowei's as he shielded Eleanor from imminent danger. No matter how many enemies they faced, his eyes burned with determination as he fought on.

There's no way they can get out of this on their own. Guowei and Soo-Young are putting their lives on the line—I need to intervene before things go too far! the prince thought to himself.

"Mum!" Jung Hwa roared, announcing his presence. "We have the signet ring, so why are we unnecessarily killing innocent people? This needs to stop!"

"I figured you would try to intervene," Angeline said flatly. "Confine him."

"But Your Highness," a guard reasoned, "your son wears the ring. It would be against protocol if we were to confine—"

With a swift loud gunshot, she mercilessly killed the man who had dared to have the audacity to question her command. As his body hit the floor, all watched in horror. She held her gun up high. "Anyone else wants to join him? *CONFINE JUNG HWA, AND DON'T LET HIM INTERVENE!* How dare anyone defy me?" Without hesitation, the guards nearby complied.

"Get off me!" Jung Hwa directed. "I command you to get off me immediately!"

Still pinning him to the ground, the two guards apologized profusely. "I'm sorry, sir, but I can't afford to lose my life. I'm a single dad," said one.

"Please don't make this harder than it needs to be, sir," said the other, forcing the boy's arms painfully behind his back before cuffing him.

Guardsmen swarmed the area as the prince was subdued, outnumbering the trio that continued to fight despite the odds stacked against them. Empress Angeline barked orders from the safety of the human barrier that had been created, blocking the only exit. "Do whatever it takes to the others, but keep the girl alive!"

Shots were fired, and screams of agony echoed through the hall. After knocking out the first minion, Guowei begins to take the gun from his holster, but a bullet hits him. He slowly looks down to see he has been shot. His head slightly turns, as if attempting to look back at Elle, but he stumbles backward and falls into Elle's arms instead, holding his stomach. Elle was horrified, seeing his shot was fatal, as she sat helplessly on the floor between her fallen friend Soo-Young and first love, knowing that Guowei's life was, too quickly coming to an end. As she grieved for them both, she hysterically cried out their names without avail.

As blood began to pool on the floor, Eleanor was losing what little hope she had left. Crying over Guowei's body, she continued hitting his chest. "Wake up, please! You promised everything would be okay, Guowei, you promised! Please don't leave me!"

Elle's tear-stained face looked down into the face of a weakened and defenseless Guowei, meeting his eyes. "Shh, don't cry . . . I'm sorry, Elle, but you must not give up now. Don't let Soo-Young's and my death be in vain. Don't let them win . . . take back your birthright."

"You put too much faith in me. How can I when I'm only one person?" she wept.

Guowei glanced down at the bracelet that encircled the young girl's wrist, knowing soon she'd have to fight alone. In his dying last breaths, he gives her his final advice. "Hey," he whispers while touching her cheek, "you know what your bracelet says? It says 'Courageous.' Having courage is the cure for one's fear, and having faith is what moves one forward. So be courageous, and have faith in yourself. Take this gun and use it wisely . . . there's only a few bullets left. Aim and shoot with both hands." Feeling his consciousness fading, he placed the loaded weapon in her hands, enclosing her fingers around it. "I don't have much time left . . ."

"You knew this would happen, didn't you?" Guowei only smiled in response, confirming her suspicion. Elle shook her head in disbelief as she began to tremble. Tears flowing freely down her cheeks, she kissed his forehead as his eyes grew heavy. "Guowei Qi, I love you."

Unable to form a final sentence, his voice trailed off, *"I love . . ."*

The man once known as Guowei Qi had expired, oxygen no longer flowing through his body.

Accepting his terrible fate, a feeling of grief and anger coursed through Elle's veins. Too many lives have been lost and much blood spilled over the past few days. Alone, she was determined to put an end to things by her own hand.

More sounds of senseless violence pulled Elle from her immense grief as she lifted her head to find its source. Down the corridor Jung Hwa was being brutally beaten, one guard accidentally dislocating one of the prince's arms as they forcefully tried to take him away to heaven knows where. Her brother's yelps echoed off the bloodied walls as he was dragged back upstairs.

"LET HIM GO!" a voice cried. Attention shifted back to an armed Elle standing on the other side of the human barrier the guards created. Gun aimed at the empress, her hands shook as she tried to keep the weapon steady. "Release my brother, NOW."

Slightly impressed by the young girl's courage, the empress let out an amused *humph. This girl lost some of her closest supporters, yet how is she still standing? How does the lowly child not tremble in fear amid such circumstances?*

"I think I've had enough excitement for one day. You're not going to shoot me, Eleanor. We both know deep down, you don't have what it takes."

Pulling the trigger, Elle's arms shot up, missing her target.

"Exactly. Bring her to me."

Wailing in pain, the guards forcefully grabbed Elle by her arms, grip tightening the more she fought and screamed. Suddenly, a gray-headed man walked to Angeline's side dressed in a white doctor's coat. In his hand was a rectangular box.

"Ah, doctor, so nice of you to finally join us. I'm assuming this is the anesthetic you were working on so diligently?"

"It is, my empress," the man said.

"Why don't we test it out? I have the perfect subject here."

Elle's eyes widened in fear as her head was forced to the side, baring her neck. "Mum, please don't do it!" the girl's brother pleaded.

"Please, don't kill me!" Elle pleaded. "If it's the throne you want, you can have it. Just let me go home! I promise not to say anything!"

Angeline got close to her prey, whispering in her ear, "That's the thing: I already have the throne. I'm not going to kill you—I like seeing you suffer alive. Where you're going, you'll wish you were dead." Stabbing a syringe into her neck, Elle began to succumb to the foreign substance entering her body. "Now rest up—you have a long journey ahead. Good night, dear."

Once incapacitated, the dethroned princess was carried onto a foreign aircraft with an unknown destination. A group of men with tanned complexions and the aroma of oud shook hands with Angeline on the tarmac, beginning a new alliance.

"Thank you for surrendering the girl. I'm sure His Highness will be pleased with her presence."

"I hope both of our nations can continue to prosper peacefully with each other."

Exchanging farewells, Angeline left Eleanor's fate in the hands of the foreign men climbing into the mysterious aircraft. Moments later the white private jet began to ascend, embarking on its journey back to their homeland beyond the vast sea.

Discover Eleanor Aurora Yamamoto's fate in the second book of The Princess Chronicles: *The Prince of Helis and Me.*

ACKNOWLEDGMENTS

Dear Reader,

If you've made it this far, thanks for allowing me to take you on this journey as you experience Elle evolve. Eleanor Aurora Aladessani-Yamamoto was a character I first imagined when I was in my sophomore year of high school.

Reading and writing have always been my form of escape. I'd always looked forward to opening my Word document on my school laptop and allowing my imagination to run wild. Fairytales filled with drama, romance, and adventure always intrigued me growing up, and they still do to this day. I hope to bring you the same joy reading Chrysanthemum Palace and hope that you continue to follow Eleanor on her path to self-discovery in the second installment of the Princess Eleanor Chronicles.

To all the people who helped me accomplish and believe in my goals, thank you from the bottom of my heart. To my family, I love you very much. Thank you for encouraging me to not give up. To Mr. Wilson, my 6th and 7th grade history teacher, thank you for showing me that there's a big world out there to explore. You will always be my favorite teacher. A special thanks to my grandfather, a fellow writer and poet, who inspired me to write from a very young age. It's thanks to you that I've found my spark.

Thanks, Mum and Dad, for supporting me throughout my endeavors (which was not always easy, I'm sure)!

And finally, again thanks to YOU, my readers! I hope we'll meet again soon.

Much love,
Morgana Sinclayr

www.ingramcontent.com/pod-product-compliance
Ingram Content Group UK Ltd.
Pitfield, Milton Keynes, MK11 3LW, UK
UKHW042014190726
13854UKWH00005B/2281